DORMANDO TOWERS

The Army of the Stronghold

ARJUN MITTAL

INDIA • SINGAPORE • MALAYSIA

ISBN 979-8-89277-892-3

Note: This book contains some funny words because of certain characters (like the goblins). Do not be confused, as a sentence like "my sword" could be "me sword" and "your heads" may become "yer heads" or "those creatures" might be "them creatures" and so forth…

Dormando Towers 2: The Army of the Stronghold

Goblin: Fiddlin

Students: Marcus, Robbert, Prith, Scabber, Flipa, Mar, Malop, Tippy and Pierce

Teachers: Headmaster Lyonis, Mrs. Bertus, Mr. Dickens, Mr. Man, Mrs. Cup, Mr. Larry, Mr. Darry, Mr. Dram and Mr. Vlad

Goblin Chieftains: Kragg, Crooked, Ivy, Tootha, Peregrines, Dagger, Rave, Lobje, Tudar and Stoup

Vampire Councilors: Rackor, Vade, Greef, Sharip and Wusim

The story goes forth

Contents

Contents

Part 1

The Coming of the Stronghold

1

Awakening

It was a gloomy day in the plains and mountains of Karabor. Relf lizards were scuttling in the sand, while renocentamins were on the shore, drinking the cool sea water. Filch snakes were slithering in the caverns and holes, seeking food and crystals. The cacti that covered the land stood still and straight, without any movement. Meanwhile, a group of mountain trolls crossed the desert to get to their habitat.

Suddenly, a castle could be seen in the distance. It was rusty grey and had gigantic walls, almost eight feet thick and 16 feet tall. Turrets and watchtowers were visible. It seemed very much like a castle, yet not quite. This was the only structure visible in Karabor, and it seemed impossible to break through. According to legend, many had tried, only to be found flat on the ground with their blood splattered all around. Would you like to know the name of this castle? Well, it is the mighty Stronghold!

* * *

"Shut it, Ivy!" Crooked the goblin croaked. "You ruddy frog, why don't you shut up!" yelled Ivy, the goblin. "Filch Slug! Hardy old Hag! Bogey drinking poo! Pinhead! Hairy swan! You, slimy wombat!" the two went on, till…

"Enough! Stop your nonsense this moment Crooked Boghead and Ivy Ornaffk! You are formidable goblins, tough commanders! Is this your destiny? Fighting each other! Stop drooping Ivy, and stop whimpering Crooked," boomed Kragg the goblin-ogre, King of the Stronghold, Ruler of Karabor. He whacked Ivy on the back with his enormous staff. Ivy straightened up immediately. He gave Crooked a very nasty look. Crooked immediately went from whimpering to nodding.

"Sit up straight!" Kragg shouted, when he saw Ivy drooping again. Kragg, along with the other nine goblin chieftains, was seated in the grand War Room, conducting the daily meeting. "Now, if I may ask, do any of you have a clue about any recent disturba…" Before he could finish, a scout barged in, "Lord Kragg," he said, urgently. "There has been a disturbance," he said. "Just what I was asking… What may be the disturbance?" asked Kragg, now annoyed.

* * *

"Let me get this straight. You're telling me that two children and a gold dragon defeated Vampire Overlord Drador and his evil goons?" asked Kragg, looking surprised and confused. "Ye… yes, my lord. The scouts who were patrolling the land of Necropolis brought me the news. There now stands a bright castle without many bones to be found. The place is infested with humans! The scouts got a good look, but did not dare attack, because of the many turrets and barracks around," explained the scout.

"The scouts predicted what might have happened and even saw the gold dragon. Good skills those scouts have…," the scout continued. "Hmmmm… This is grand information and I thank you, goblin," said Kragg. "Oh! you're truly welcome sire, and another thi…," the goblin continued, but Kragg interrupted. "Stop, we can hear the rest later. Hurry along now, for I have an important discussion to start." With a low bow, the goblin hurried out of the room.

When there was no one but Kragg and the other chieftains in the room, he started sharing his thoughts. "What those scouts concluded, about those children and a gold dragon killing Drador, is impossible. Drador the Vampire Overlord is one of the most powerful creatures in the world. He cannot be defeated, and definitely not by two children and a stupid old dragon," he said. "I do wonder though what happened to Drador," said Kragg. "Then how can he be defeated, milord?" asked Crooked, still frightened after the last beating from Kragg. Kragg looked suspiciously at Crooked. "Well, the only way, from what others say, is if the greatest sword strikes him down. It has an extremely long blade. Its handle is covered in jewels and diamonds. Its sharp point can cut a finger even if one touches it gently. Can any of you tell me the name of the sword?" asked Kragg. "The Heartstealer!" answered Lobje, the goblin. "Yes, Lobje is correct," nodded Kragg.

"Sadly, no one knows where it is. Some people think it is in Hell Fall. Lost. But others think it was destroyed during the last battle," explained Kragg. "But why does it help sire?" asked Tootha. "Oh! That sword has some history with Drador, I think. It is said that in the battle of the four armies, R and M struck Drador with it. Drador lost half his life that day, but he was not finished. With all his might, he blew the whole battlefield with the darkest magic. Not a single creature even from his own army survived, except him. He saw the sword beside him. He cursed it and sent it flying in the air, surrounded by flames. It is said that he fears that one day the sword will return and strike him again, and blow the other half of his life away…," finished Kragg. All the goblins looked terrified, but they seemed to have understood.

"Well, that is not all. Another artifact that was used in that same battle was the Totem of Absorption," said Kragg. "It gives the user such defense, that only someone like a god can cause harm. And Drador, well, had God-like powers," explained Kragg. "Oh! And how did the Totem help that day?" asked Tootha. "Oh! Do any of you read history?" asked Kragg, annoyed. None of them nodded. "Fine, but I'm getting tired of this. Our meeting is turning into a history lesson," continued Kragg. "That day, R and M activated the Totem after finding it and used it. It was the only reason they were able to reach Drador in the end. Without the Totem, they would have died on their way to him. Drador's army was not a couple of skeletons and zombies, it was more like legions of them. Hordes of dark creatures were involved, such as Cerebri, Bone Dragons, Dark Knights and, I think, Necromancy Reapers...," explained Kragg, trying to recall history.

Everyone was trying to follow what their king was saying. "Well, that is that. I think we are..." Before he could finish, an excited Ivy said, "Wait! Sire! A very important thing! What if we steal this... Totem! Won't it be useful?" Now Kragg looked like he was about to explode. "I AM OUTRAGED! DO NONE OF YOU KNOW WHAT WOULD HAPPEN IF WE GOT **OUR** HANDS ON IT?" thundered Kragg. The goblins were startled, some even fell off their chairs. Kragg was panting. Tudar, Kragg's most trusted goblin, walked over to Kragg and helped him calm down and get back into his chair. Once all the goblins got back into their seats, Kragg continued. "I am sorry my fellow chieftains. I lost my temper because none of you know the history. Goblins like you should have read the whole series of Knowledge of Arabon," apologized Kragg. "I will continue now. About two, thousand years ago, Lord Ren of the Stronghold, as you know, was very good friends with a cartographer who lived in Goblin Market, down the road.

The cartographer, however, was not in the mood for a happy relationship... One day, the cartographer found the holy map of the Totem. In the past, goblins had uncovered its location, along with other forces, such as demons from Hell Fall, but they all knew the history as well," explained Kragg.

"You see, the cartographer also knew history. Only true heroes like R or M could use such an artifact, but the cartographer knew that Ren was a lazy goblin, so he hatched a plan to betray his friend.

"The next day, when they met, the cartographer showed Ren the map. Unable to control his greed, Ren snatched it. Without wasting any time, he rounded up a few other goblin guards to journey with him on his quest to find the Totem of Absorption. It was not in Karabor, but on an island, so he purchased a ship and set sail…" read Kragg, from a history book. "After several days at sea, Ren discovered the island. On it was a small cavern, and Ren thought the Totem might be hidden in it." Kragg took a little pause to catch his breath.

"Once Ren entered the cavern, he ordered the guards to wait outside, as he feared they might steal the Totem for themselves. For a few minutes, Ren walked inside the cavern, looking for the Totem, until he saw a bright glow in a tiny water stream. He looked a little closer and saw its details. The Totem was right in front of his eyes. Ren cried with joy, so loudly, that the guards thought something was wrong and hurried into the cave. Ren grabbed the Totem. For a few moments, nothing happened, until Ren was suddenly electrified, as if struck by a thunderbird. There was a lot a crackling and screaming as Ren was electrified to death.

The guards found him on the floor, still crackling. They saw the Totem fall back into the stream of water. They quickly carried Ren out of the cave. That was how Lord Ren of the Stronghold met his fate," explained Kragg, who was now looking like a potato, because he was so tired. "But sire, in the end, why could goblins or devils not touch the Totem?" asked Stoup.

"Well, again, 6,000 years ago, when the Totem was forged by the elves of Frohaven, it was protected by a powerful spell. It became an artifact to be held and used only for the greater good. Beings who were kind and thoughtful were the ones who could use it, not devils, ogres, goblins, vampires, or… any sort of Darkness," explained Kragg, who was looking sleepy a few moments back, but now seemed rejuvenated.

"Ah, yes, I am now concerned about the council of Necropolis, for they must have fled from Necropolis Land Fall after the humanoids took over," said Kragg.

"Lobje, order the scouts to get into their boats and sail all around Karabor, for I need more information about Necropolis Land Fall. The council will definitely have more information," said Kragg. "Yes, Milord," said Lobje, and exited the room.

2

The New Towers

A bright, sunny day dawned over Necropolis Land Fall. Yes, that does sound ridiculous, but a spell had been cast over the land long before the present. In the presence of any creature who meant harm, the land would turn pitch dark. Thunder, lightning, and rain would follow instantly. But, in the absence of darkness and evil, the opposite would happen… the sky would remain bright and sunny.

Now, the reason why it was bright and sunny was because the people of Dormando had all slowly sailed towards Necropolis Land Fall, where there was no village, markets, farms, forgers or even an inn. The people of Dormando came up with a very creative plan… to build a village for themselves. It took a few months, but in the end they were very proud of what they had created. Yet, something bothered them. Bones. Lots and lots of bones scattered over the land. The people realized that the bones still brought darkness to them. For months, they cleaned the whole of Necropolis. When there were no bones to be seen, the land became bright. In fact, the brightest thing to be seen was the new castle. Well, it was still the same old Necropolis castle, but it was painted a bright white, the opposite of what it used to be, pure black.

New towers were being built around the castle, to make space for more classrooms. If you walked down the path to the castle, you would see a small white tent. It was ugly and pale, but no one really cared about that, for what was inside was far more interesting. Inside that tent sat eight children, with sleeping bags and a chess board…

"Checkmate!" called Tippy, who was playing a game of chess with Malop. "Ugh, this is boring," muttered Malop, feeling ridiculous about losing. It was seven-thirty in the morning, and the boys had just woken up. Tippy and Malop were setting up the chess board for another game, because Malop insisted on a rematch. The other boys were lying on their blankets, staring into space. "Hmph, I wonder why Headmaster Lyonis put us in this tent? We've spent two whole days in here, playing chess and talking about stuff," said Marcus. "Yeah, they're probably planning some big announcement, which will most certainly be boring," agreed Robbert. "Yes, I do remember our first year, where they did the same thing, and in the end it was just a boring announcement of a new staff member in school, which happened to be Mr. Dickens, the most boring English teacher in history," added Scabber. The other boys all nodded, except for Marcus, who pressed one ear against the tent. He could hear some shuffling and the sound of someone walking about. He could also hear the banging of a hammer. "Can you hear that?" asked Marcus. All the other students pressed their ears against the tent as well. "Oh yeah! What's that shuffling? There's like a bunch of feet moving!" exclaimed Mar. "Agreed, but there's also this banging noise. Maybe an axe? No, a hammer really," added Robbert.

Soon, the boys forgot about the noise and turned their attention to the game between Malop and Tippy. Tippy was clearly winning, but Malop was putting up quite a fight. After Tippy won, Marcus challenged him to a game and won! One thing they all agreed to was, the winner of each game will stay and play against another person. Marcus beat everyone in the end…

After hours of chess, the boys again heard loud footsteps really close to their tent. "Ah! I think someone has come to take us out of this stupid tent," said Tippy, relieved. That very moment, Headmaster Lyonis untied the knot used to secure the tent and pulled open the canvas. "Good morning students, it is finally time for you to exit this tent," he said. "Good morning, Headmaster Lyonis," the students said. The boys got up from the grassy floor and carried their sleeping bags and chess board in their hands. They followed Lyonis to the main path.

"I am sorry that you had to live in the tent for a couple of days, but it will be worth it. You'll see," explained Headmaster Lyonis as they continued to walk up the path.

"It's an announcement, isn't it?" asked Tippy. "Well, partially, but not quite," answered Headmaster Lyonis. The boys looked a bit pleased.

After a while, the castle came into sight. At first, the boys saw it as the regular structure, but, as they got closer, they saw a much larger version of the castle. Many more towers had been built around the bright white castle. Other small structures, such as huts, had been built too, and they seemed to be reserved for classes. "Wow, this is amazing!" exclaimed some students. "Stupendous!" cried the others.

"Yes, yes, I'm, sure you all like this very much, but another surprise awaits," added the headmaster. The students could not see the gates of the castle, so they continued walking. Before them, stood a crowd of children wearing uniforms. "Forty-two new students have joined our school," said Headmaster Lyonis. The former eight students were gawping. They never expected the school to have more children. They looked on with glee, and beamed in excitement. (Even Tippy).

Later that eventful day, 50 students gathered in the main hall, which also seemed to be bigger than it was before. Marcus, Robbert, Prith, Scabber, Flipa, Mar, Malop and Tippy were seated in a row of chairs right in front of the teachers' podium. Their chairs were placed such that they could see all the students too.

"Now before you go to your dorms, I would like to make a few announcements," said the headmaster, who was standing behind the lectern.

"Firstly, I would like to introduce our staff. I am Headmaster Lyonis. Feel free to call me just headmaster. Next, is our wonderful history teacher, Mrs. Bertus," he said. Mrs. Bertus blushed. "We also have Mr. Man, whom you could also call Professor Mandelaiin.

He will be teaching you geography. Mr. Dickens is your English teacher. He will make sure you learn to speak English fluently. Next up is our art teacher, Mrs. Cup. She has studied the different art forms in Dormandian history and has agreed to teach them to you all this year," continued the headmaster. "Larry here is the librarian. Any book you borrow from the library, Larry will not forget, so return them on time, or you'll see his dark side! Darry here, who also happens to be Larry's brother, is the chef. He will keep you all healthy at Dormando Towers," announced the headmaster. The students clapped, then waited for the headmaster to introduce the remaining two teachers.

"This year, we have two new staff members. Firstly, I'd like to introduce Dram. He will be our caretaker and keep our castle clean. He will also help us teachers in our daily tasks, for he is a very helpful man," said the headmaster. Dram was stout and didn't look very happy about being a caretaker. In fact, he looked worried. "Finally, there is Sir Vlad Valor," said the headmaster. A serious but sharp looking man with a sword on his back. He looked as if he was on his way to war. "Vlad will teach you how to protect yourselves. You may call it self-defense class. This year, he will teach you how to handle basic weapons, such as swords and bows and arrows." The students suddenly looked very excited. Battling with swords and bows seemed exciting. Certainly not a usual class (or boring for that matter).

"Now, you may think this class will be fun and enjoyable, but the point is to prepare you to fight off dangers that may come your way in the future," added the headmaster. The students nodded quietly.

"As you know, this very school was taken over by vampires last term. This class will prepare you to defend yourselves in such instances," he chipped in. A lot of whispers suddenly echoed around the room.

"Oh! And two of our eight former students saved our school from those wicked vampires. Marcus and Robbert. I expect they will do well in Sir Vlad Valor's class this year," the headmaster continued. Sir Vlad looked closely at Marcus and Robbert. "For the self-defense class, outside on the school grounds, is a weapon house. You may use these weapons only during Sir Vlad's class. Entrance to the house is otherwise restricted. Also, there has been a small addition of a… dungeon," concluded Headmaster Lyonis. The students gasped even as the headmaster looked uneasy. "Now, the dungeon is only constructed for safety purposes. Students are strictly forbidden from the dungeon, and there will be consequences if you break this rule," he said sternly. Then, Headmaster Lyonis concluded, "I wish you all a good and exciting year ahead. You may exit and find your dormitories. Classes will begin tomorrow, however, today you may spend time with your friends and have a restful day. As you were…"

The students rushed out of the main hall, looking for their dormitories. Everyone was excited to make new friends. Marcus, Robbert, Prith, Scabber, Flipa, Mar, Malop and Tippy headed back to their old dorm to meet the new student there. "I hope we get someone like us," said Malop as the group climbed up the staircase to the third-floor corridor. "Yeah, I have a feeling we'll get someone good," agreed Robbert. The boys hurried up the staircase…

3

The Decision of the Council

Lord Kragg, King of the Stronghold, was seated on his enormous throne made of gold, in his private room. He was waiting for the scouts, who were ordered to seek the council of Necropolis and bring them back to the Stronghold. It had been a week and Kragg was clearly impatient. He thought a lot about the questions he would ask the council. The vampires in the council of Necropolis were quite powerful and had served in the battle of the four armies. Suddenly, there was loud knocking on the door. KNOCK! KNOCK! KNOCK! "You may enter," said Kragg. For a few moments, there was silence. Then, the door creaked open, and Lobje the goblin stepped into the room. "Ah! Lobje. What brings you here?" asked Kragg. "Good morning, sire, I have come to tell yeh some grand news," answered Lobje. "Well, what is it? Is it to do with…" Before he could finish, a scout yelled as he barged into the room, "Lord Kragg!" He was the same scout who had interrupted the meeting the other day. "One more time you do that, and I'll feed you to the wolves!" scolded Kragg. The scout looked a bit pale. "Sorry Milord, but…"

"Oh! And next time, knock. This is a private room, you fool!" interrupted Kragg.

"I am truly sorry, Milord, but this is urgent! The scouts have returned!" exclaimed the scout. Suddenly, Kragg's face broke into a grin. Lobje scowled at the scout, as he wanted to deliver the news to Kragg himself. "Excellent! What news have they brought? Have they found the council's hiding spot?" demanded Kragg excitedly.

"Ah! Yes sir, I have a feeling you will like what they have found. If you will just follow me down to the visitor's hall…"

* * *

"Let go of me, ugly toad! Yes, gerr'off me!" Five dark figures, all handcuffed, were being taken to the visitor's hall to be questioned by Lord Kragg. Three guards were holding them in line, restricting them from escaping. Once they reached the hall, the guards threw them in and shut the door. The five figures struggled but managed to get up and sit on their knees. A few moments later, Kragg, Lobje and the scout entered the room. Kragg and Lobje recognized the set instantly. The council of Necropolis was seated before them.

"R… remove t… the h… handcuffs," demanded Kragg. The guards did as they were told. Then, the council looked up at Kragg. "Ah! Lord Kragg, King of the Stronghold, ruler of Karabor, am I right?" asked one of the councilors. "Indeed, I am the great ruler of this land," agreed Kragg, suspiciously. "Well, please tell us why you have commanded us here?" asked the same member, who seemed to speak for everyone in the council. "I have a few questions for you. Necropolis things, which I could not answer myself," answered Kragg.

"The name's Rackor. Leader of the council of Necropolis. I have the vampire councilors, Vade, Greef, Sharip and Wusim with me. A few of our fellow councilors did not survive the perilous journey escaping from Necropolis land fall," explained Rackor. "Do ye' mind if we take a seat before ye' question us?" asked Greef, the vampire. "Not at all, there are a few chairs in the corner," said Kragg and pointed to a group of chairs. Vade the vampire whispered some spell to move the chairs to them, but nothing happened. He repeated them…

"Oh, don't try and use magic here. It doesn't work in the Stronghold. Actually, in most of Karabor," added Kragg. The vampires groaned and waddled to the corner of the room to grab a chair each. Once they returned, Kragg asked, "Firstly, did you know that Drador the vampire overlord is thought to be dead?" Rackor answered, "Of course, we were aware of that, but only a fool would believe that." "Agreed, but do you have any idea where he might be headed, or how he came to be suspected dead?" questioned Kragg. "Well, why should we tell you that?" demanded Rackor. "Well, maybe if we knew where he was, all forces of evil could join hands and bring the age of men crashing down!" yelled Kragg, slightly annoyed. The vampires were quite startled, but had to agree with Kragg. "Very well, you have made a point," sighed Rackor.

"Our visions and powers have spoken to us. There is a small island in the sea, near Hell Fall. It seems Drador is currently stranded there. He seems to have fainted…," said Rackor. "Like that's going to help us," muttered Kragg. "Wait, there is more. Our vision tells us that after waking up he will find his way to Hell Fall and partner with the devils themselves," added Rackor. Lobje, who was still seated next to Kragg, looked up at Kragg confused.

Kragg's eyes remained fixed on the vampires. "It is exactly what I suspected. Centuries after the battle of the four armies, evil will join forces once more. Ruled by one. Drador. To have the men destroyed, or rather all things on the side of good. Once again, the father above shall fall. Evil will rule the world," murmured Kragg. No one spoke for a few moments. "Well, if you do not mind Lord Kragg, I have a suggestion," said Rackor. "Go ahead. We could do with them at this moment," replied Kragg. "I say…" paused Rackor, "that we overrun the school."

The scout gasped. Kragg looked very confused.

"School? What school? Is this some sort of joke?" asked Kragg. Rackor pointed at the scout, "I think your scout knows which school I am talking about." Kragg's eyes turned towards the scout, who now looked like he was about to explode.

"W… well, Milord, I was going to tell you this, but you…" Before he could finish, Kragg yelled, "Leave us!" The terrified scout darted out of the room, whimpering. No one spoke while Kragg continued to curse the scout under his breath. "That goblin won't be in Karabor much longer…," he muttered. When he calmed down, he said, "Tell me more about this school." Rackor explained, "When Drador and his servants took over the school, it was located in the main castle. They kidnapped the students, and took them to Necropolis. The main castle of Necropolis then became the school. That is the school we are talking about."

"Now I understand! But how has the castle of Necropolis changed?" asked Kragg. "After Drador was thought to be killed, the humans turned our grand estate castle 'school' into their human school. They basically made Necropolis their home! What's more, a village has come up around it," answered Rackor. Kragg took a few minutes to think of a counter question. "Very well, but why do we need to overrun the school?" he asked. "We need revenge! Our castle, our home, is not supposed to be a school. For centuries, it has been home to Necropolis' vampires!" answered Wusim. "I do understand, but how does this matter to the beings of Karabor. There is no connection," said Kragg. "Oh! Yes, there is a connection, Kragg," said Rackor. "Our instincts have told us more. The Dormandian people will soon join forces with the people of Frohaven, who plan to take down Hell Fall and Karabor. Do you have any idea how large the army of Frohaven is? Almost as large as the army in the battle of the Four Armies! Add to that a few angels and a couple of dragons and their horde of crusaders, Karabor will be gone," said Rackor.

"And how may I trust you?" asked Kragg. "Vampires are cursed when they are born. If they stir up a lie, they die," said Rackor. "Oh! That's good enough for me," sighed Kragg. "Oh yes, surely milord." croaked Rackor of course lying at the very moment, but Kragg was too gullible to notice with his peanut-sized brain. "What may be your plan? We can't go with a couple of sticks to take down a whole castle," asked Kragg. Rackor started thinking.

"First, we need an army. A fourth of your goblin army will do. Around a thousand or two of them, quarter of them archers. Then we need five ogres and five trolls to guard the army from the rear. Maybe eight cyclops to destroy the huge structures? They will be posted on the tall towers, on top of the renocentamins. Another renocentamin will carry a grand carriage with you and us in it. We shall also take four… behemoths," finished Rackor. Kragg was astonished. He had never let the behemoths out of Karabor, since there were only a limited number in Karabor.

"Very well," agreed Kragg. Rackor grinned. "Well, what may be the attack plan?" asked Kragg. "First, we will take the warships across Arabon. Three to four days shall it take to reach Necropolis, depending on how fast we move. Once we arrive there, we will circle the shores to the east side of Dormandian Necropolis Land Fall, where there are no watchtowers," continued Rackor. "Once we descend from the ships, we will march to the village, destroying everything in our way, including the humans. After the massacre, we will move towards the castle and the cyclops will launch their boulders at it, destroying it completely," explained Rackor. "So, do we intend to kill the humans in the castle?" asked Kragg. "No. We will capture as many children and teachers as we can and bring them back to Karabor. Then, we must question them about what they have seen and think about Drador. Hopefully, we can capture the ones who thought they destroyed Drador. We need these answers before we reclaim our home," concluded Rackor. "Good. The army will be ready in a day. The plan and news shall be spread too," added Kragg. "You vampires may rest in the hammock cabin for visitors. It's the room below this one," Kragg said. "Very well, Lord Kragg, the decision has been made!" said Rackor. Lord Kragg and Councilor Rackor shook hands.

———•◉•———

4

New Friends and New Foes

Marcus, Robbert and the six other former students went to their dorm to meet the new student, hoping to make some new friends. When they opened the door, they saw a boy their age, putting his luggage on his new bunk bed. "Oh! Hello! I think you must be new here. Would you like to introduce yourself?" asked Robbert. The new boy turned to see the eight students. "Oh! Hello! My name is Pierce William Shillingworth. I'm very excited to be sharing this dorm with the eight former students of the school," he said. "Glad to meet you. I'm Robbert. I have Marcus, my best friend, here. Malop, Scabber, Prith, Tippy, Flipa and Mar are here too," continued Robbert. Later, Marcus, Robbert and the other six, showed Pierce around the dorm. They showed him all the secret places and gave him important tips. They also showed him how to get off his bed without falling and breaking his bones, since he was on the topmost bunk. The boys spent the rest of the day talking with Pierce and playing chess. Pierce said that he didn't know how to play chess, so it took the boys a long time explaining the rules to him.

At night, they ate their dinner and went to bed early. They spent some time talking to Pierce because about all the teachers and classes that they thought were the best.

* * *

The next day, after breakfast, the boys headed to the fields near the weapons house for their first term's first lesson. Self Defense. The boys chattered on, as they were very excited about this class. When they arrived in the fields, they found a row of chairs. They took their seats and waited for Sir Vlad to arrive. A few moments later, they saw him descend from the weapons house with a dozen swords and bows, and stacks of twigs. "Greetings to you all. My name is Sir Vlad Valor. You may call me Mr. Vlad," said Vlad. "We will start by selecting a weapon for each of you. Let us start with you, my boy," Vlad said, pointing at Malop.

Malop walked up to Vlad. "Which weapon do you want to use? A sword, or a bow?" asked Vlad. "Erm… I prefer a sword as I feel it might be easier to use, Mr. Vlad," answered Malop. "Very good. I myself am an expert with one. Take the blunt sword. We won't be using very long and sharp swords, as this is your first time," said Vlad. Tippy was called up next. "I will take a bow, Mr. Vlad. I've had a bit of practice before. My dad used to be an archer before he hurt his arm and changed his work to become a master of the forges…" said Tippy. "Okay. Interesting. Take the short bow. It seems to be just the right size for you, eh," said Vlad. Flipa was followed by Mar, Prith, Scabber, Pierce, Marcus and Robbert. Marcus and Robbert chose swords straightaway. "Now, those with swords, stand together," said Vlad, pointing to the side of the field that had large rocky pillars. "Those with bows, stand on the other side that has stands and wooden plates," he said. The pillars were cheap dummies, and the wooden plates were quickly made targets.

The students with the bows got sharp thin twigs instead of arrows. Vlad taught the students who had chosen swords to hold them properly. He swung his sword next to one of the dummies. That was a standard way of striking with a sword. When he thought they were ready, he showed the students with bows, how much to pull back a bow, and how high to hold the bow, according to different targets.

Dong! Dong! Dong! The bell rang, which meant it was time for the next class. When the bell rang four times, it meant that it was time for lunch. "In the next class, tomorrow, we will discuss the legends of battle. For now, hurry on to your next classes," said Vlad. The students put their weapons down and hurried away…

* * *

Later in the day, the nine boys were sitting at the lunch table eating and chatting. Malop, as usual, took his favorite food, sauteed vegetables. Marcus asked the new student, "So, Pierce, where do you come from?" Pierce said he lived in the village. "Me too!" exclaimed Marcus. Flipa went next, "I don't live in the village. My dad is a swordsman like Mr. Vlad. I live in the Knights inn." Marcus was surprised to hear this. "Wow! You never told us that. It also explains why Robbert and I couldn't find you during the last holidays. We wanted to show you our new chess set so we knocked on a lot of people's doors," explained Marcus. "Oh, sorry about that," apologized Flipa. "I do not come from the village either," said Tippy. "Here we go again…" sighed Marcus. "I live in an enormous house next to the village. My parents work at the biggest forge in town. They even own the statue of Sir Dormando!" exclaimed Tippy. "Wow. Amazing!" said Pierce, smiling at Tippy.

After lunch, they headed to the dorm for their break. Concentrating on a full stomach was quite difficult, so they didn't have a class immediately. Robbert, Tippy, Malop, Pierce and Flipa played chess, while Prith, a bit sick after lunch, lay on his bed. Marcus, Scabber and Mar went the library. While Scabber and Mar headed for the Legends of Battles section, Marcus explored the Monsters and Creatures section, where he found a pile of rather fat books.

"Mythical creatures, no… Magnificent creatures, no… The creatures of the dead, no… none of this is new.

Wait… The Creatures of the Land of Karabor?" muttered Marcus as he browsed through the book. He knew about Karabor, as it was one of the lands of the world. "Hmmmm…" He looked at the cover that had a terrifying, wicked-looking goblin on it.

The book was old and dusty and seemed like it wasn't supposed to be there as it didn't have the stamp of Dormando Towers. "*It wasn't written by the Lords of Dormando?*" wondered Marcus, then realized the book had no author. "Interesting…," murmured Marcus. He headed over to where Scabber and Mar were. They were discussing legends, when Marcus interrupted, "Hey guys, I'm ready to go if you are." The two boys nodded and waved Larry goodbye.

On their way back, Marcus looked at his book. Instead of the author's name, there was ragged marks. From what Marcus could make out, there were letters that spelt K-R-A-G-G. *"Kragg?"* thought Marcus, "But who is Kragg?" Once they reached the dormitory, Scabber and Mar headed to a corner to talk about their books, while Marcus joined the game of chess. He decided to read his book later…

After a day of classes, including Self-defense, Art, Geography and English, the boys had a grand meal, which sent them drooping back to their beds. "Oh! I don't feel very good," groaned Marcus. "Me neither," moaned Malop. They all hurried towards their beds, climbing the ladders as quickly as possible, to get into their cozy, warm beds. As they settled down, Tippy did his usual honors, "Have a nightmare!" A surprised Pierce asked, "Why would you want that?" Tippy said he didn't know and pulled the covers on himself.

Marcus, unlike the rest, was wide awake. He felt it would be best to read his book once everyone had slept. When he was sure, he lit his candle and took out the book. He opened the book and dust blew into his face. Cough! Cough! He quickly pulled his covers all the way up to his forehead in case anyone woke up. "Phew…," he said, relieved that no one had heard him. He re-opened the book again and started reading about the many different creatures. "These must be from Karabor," thought Marcus, as the start of the book had a small description about Karabor. It talked about the many mountains in the region and Marcus realized all the creatures seemed to be from mountainous areas. He read about goblins, ogres, trolls, and wolves.

Then, he came to a part of the book called the 'Stronghold. What was that supposed to mean?

In short, it was home to many, many creatures. Especially goblins. Marcus wondered what behemoths were. The description said that they were huge ape like creatures. They had claws that measured up to thirty-five centimeters! They had thick, furry skin, and an enormous overbite. "The mighty Stronghold was almost impossible to break into." He read on. "Lord Kragg, the king of the Stronghold, ruler of Karabor, said that one day he'd have the age of men come crashing down!" Marcus shouted a little too loudly. He heard snorting from Malop who must have woken up. Luckily, he turned around to fall asleep again. Marcus sighed. He couldn't go on like this. The phrase he just read alerted him that the Stronghold is a threat to humans like himself. Marcus decided he had read enough for the night. He put out his candle and slowly fell asleep.

* * *

In the morning, the students got ready for another school day… On their way to the breakfast hall, Marcus started whispering to Robbert about what he had read last night. Robbert was his best friend and almost a brother, so Marcus couldn't ever keep a secret from him. He told him all about the strange book.

"You read a book about the creatures of Karabor?" asked Robbert. "Yes. Karabor is where goblins, ogres, and other evil beings dwell," said Marcus. "I see. That's interesting, though who'd keep a book about that in here? It's unlikely a teacher did," said Robbert. "Well, yeah, I guess so. One more thing, there is this structure in Karabor called the Stronghold. It's kind of like a castle. And the king of the

Stronghold is Kragg. And Kragg has sworn that one day he will have the age of men come crashing down!" explained Marcus. Robbert stopped a moment to think.

"Well, that's interesting as well. I think that makes him our… foe?" asked Robbert. Marcus shook his head. "I think this whole 'Kragg' thing is a bunch of baloney," said Marcus. "Maybe it is, maybe it isn't. I, for one, think he's still out there," disagreed Robbert. "If only I knew. What if Kragg is out there, preparing an army to conquer us…" he wondered.

5

The Ships Descend

From the day Lord Kragg and the council of Necropolis had their meeting, the Stronghold's gigantic army had started rounding up with haste. And when it had… it was mighty. Pwaaaaa! A horn blew so loudly, the whole army could hear it. Approximately five hundred goblins marched from the Stronghold to the west of Karabor where the ships usually landed. The infantry of goblins was armed with swords. Behind them were the archers and behind the archers were five enormous ogres and five trolls who looked like they were ready to eat humans for breakfast. Behind them were, the hugest of all creatures, the behemoths. Four behemoths were as dangerous as about a hundred ogres. Their sharp twenty-four-inch claws were scraping the ground, preparing for battle.

That was not the end of it. Behind them were huge renocentamins, who carried the carriages. All the carriages, except one, were open from the top and in each one stood an enormous cyclops. Each cyclops had about ten boulders. The grand carriage housed Lord Kragg and the vampire councilors. "A fine ride this is," said Rackor the vampire. "Yes, and so it begins," said Kragg. The army was getting close to the shipyard. "Vampires, how do you feel about a ship ride, eh?" asked Kragg curiously. "Fine, yes. All we fear is the creatures in there. Nasty things dwell in the seas of Arabon," answered Rackor. No one said anything until they were in sight of the shipyard. "Go forth, the army of the Stronghold," said Kragg. "The revenge of the vampires!" Greef the vampire chipped in. Kragg frowned at Greef, and then in an instance, smiled and said, "Of course!"

There were eleven war ships to be taken to the land of Necropolis. The eight renocentamins each had a ship for themselves. Not just because they were enormous, but because they carried the cyclops on top of themselves. Goblins squeezed into any space that remained in the ships. One ship carried the renocentamin with the grand carriage that held Kragg and the vampire councilors. The last two ships were for the behemoths, trolls and ogres and remaining goblins.

Soon, the ships began to sail, steered by the goblins. As they entered deeper waters, it started to get very cold and chilly. This wasn't normal Karabor weather. The mist and fog made Kragg go, "Cooooold, isn't it? N-not n-normal weather f-for c-creatures from K-Karabor." He was shivering. "Hmm, it's almost natural weather for vampires," said Rackor, enjoying the cold. Kragg commanded one of his servants to bring him a quilt, then poked his head out into the open to see the other ships. All the creatures aboard looked like they were going to freeze in the biting cold. Sadly, there weren't enough quilts for them. "Well, I think I'm going to pop off for a while. No point in taking in these evil winds," said Kragg and slouched into the throne he sat on.

* * *

A couple of days of hard travel passed. The cold air almost froze a few cyclops on the way. Goblins were forced to find loose rigging to cover and keep the beasts warm. Kragg nodded off for ages, which happened to be a couple of days. When he got up, the vampires greeted him. "Good morning, Lord Kragg. You have been sleeping for two days straight. Pretty long for a nap, eh?" started Rackor. "Oh, really? Two days feels like an hour when I am asleep. It is natural for ogres to slumber for many moons at a stretch," said Kragg, yawning. He peeped outside the carriage to see where they were heading. A faint sight of a shore appeared. It was vast and seemed to have structures around it. "Frohaven. First land of men. Pity really, we shan't take them on, for their army will most likely be ten times the size of ours at the moment. Anyway, the behemoths would go berserk if they saw any dragons. They don't like them overgrown lizards for some strange reason," explained Kragg. The vampires nodded in agreement.

When the goblin sailors spotted Frohaven, they quickly started turning away from the shore. If even one being saw them, their entire army would be dead. They believed angels would come out of the clouds and kill all of Stronghold's creatures. And that would not be the end. They would go to Karabor next, and conquer it. The only reason Frohaven had not conquered Karabor already was that they had no idea of what the army was like. Karabor was quiet when it came to big battles. Lucky fellows, those goblins. Suddenly, the ships turned diagonally and set sail for Necropolis. They were in very deep waters, when the creatures spotted a couple of sea serpents racing through the water.

The cyclops were ordered to throw boulders at the serpents when they jumped out of the water snapping up goblins who were unaware. One enormous one leapt up and got smacked in the head before he could taste a nasty goblin.

It groaned and toppled into the sea, dead. Its skull had probably cracked. The next one was small, so one shot sent the creature flying over the waters. It was still gasping for air, when a goblin picked up a spare harpoon and threw it at the sea serpent's head. It pierced the creature's eyes and head. The creature died eventually, after a few more blows. Kragg looked menacingly cruel and let out an evil cackle. "He! ha! ha! ha!"

The ships sailed forth…

6

And the Spears Fly through the Sky (Part 1)

"Wow! I wonder why I never tried these so-called blackberries before, Marcus," said Robbert, wolfing them down. The students were finishing breakfast, when the bell went off, Dong! Dong! Dong! "Oops, time for class," said Marcus. The boys followed, as Marcus headed out of the breakfast hall. They walked to their classroom for one of their favorite lessons, History, with the wonderful Mrs. Bertus.

"Welcome, students. Good day to you. Before we begin, I'd like to introduce myself to the new students. My name is Mrs. Mallory Bertus, of Barnum Bertus. I come from these parts, just like most of you. Now, would you like to introduce yourselves?" asked Mrs. Bertus. Pierce thought about what to say, and went first. "My name is Pierce William Shillingworth, of the... Shillingworths. I am also from these vast parts," he said. "Wonderful, wonderful. Welcome to our class Pierce. I am informed that you know your fellow mates, but I like the thing of properly introducing people," said Mrs. Bertus. Marcus tried to differ, "But, but, we…"

"Okay, first up, we have Marcus Arthur Fedrick. Next, Robbert Algar Fedrick," said Mrs. Bertus, before she was interrupted by Pierce, "Sorry to interrupt miss, but I didn't know Marcus and Robbert were brothers?" asked Pierce. Marcus and Robbert glanced at each other.

"I mean, they hardly look alike," Pierce continued. "That is because we aren't brothers," said Marcus gloomily. "We are best friends, but I was taken in by Robbert's family when my father went missing." Everyone was quiet, until Pierce said, "Oh! Sorry about that."

Mrs. Bertus continued to introduce everyone in the class, till she got fed up. "Lastly, we have Tippy Ambrose Heridain," she finished. Tippy flinched when she said his middle name, as the boys sometimes laughed at it. Mar, Scabber and Prith were already sniggering in the back benches. One stern look from Mrs. Bertus shut them up.

"Well, students, it is about time we start learning. Today, we shall learn about our world. We are a part of this world, and there's no point in arguing, is there?" Mrs. Bertus explained. No one really understood what she meant but acted as if everything was true. "All the lands join to make up the world. The first land is Frohaven, in the middle. It is the home of the first men, and all your ancestors must have lived there as well." Everyone looked confused.

"But, Miss, I thought we used to live in the land of Dormando?" asked a confused Marcus. "Yes, getting to that part now. You see, a fight between two sides had occurred thousands of years before in Frohaven. The land of Dormando was not even a thing then. One part of Frohaven wanted different rules than the other half. The royal side had driven away the people who disagreed into the sea. Everyone landed up on our older land, Dormando, and made a vow to never make peace with Frohaven." she explained. "However, the rule was broken when the battle of the four armies took place, when men fought together, side by side. Of course, Frohaven isn't only the land of men. Other things dwell there, like…," she paused. Everyone waited for her to finish. "Nothing. Nothing at all," she said in a grave voice. "Well, Miss, what rules were disagreed on?" asked Scabber. "Oh, I am not going to let you into that stuff," Mrs. Bertus said. "Enough of Frohaven, let's talk about Hell Fall, the land of Saratan, the devil. No one knows if he still lives, or whether he was killed in battle. Hell Fall is said to be the most dangerous and unstable land of all. I'll give you some advice: if you meet an angel, don't ask it about Hell Fall. One word, and you will have your head in your hands. Devils and angels are arch enemies, sworn to kill each other.

"Then, we have Karabor," continued Mrs. Bertus. *Hey, that's the book I was reading!* thought Marcus. He raised his hand, before Mrs. Bertus could say another word. "Yes Marcus? Make it quick now," she said. "Miss, I have read a book about Karabor." Mrs. Bertus looked confused, but interested too.

"Very good, why don't you tell us what you read," she said. "The land of Karabor is full of mountains, some deserts, and plains. It is full of goblins, trolls, and ogres. Humanoids don't come from Karabor. The finest thing there is the Stronghold, a huge war castle. The king of the stronghold is Kragg, and he rules over Karabor. Kragg loathes humans and aspires to wipe us out from this world…" Mrs. Bertus interrupted. "Okay! That's enough Marcus! I wonder where you read such a book, anyway… forget about it, everyone. "Next we have…" Dong! Dong! Dong! "Oh, we will have to wait another day. Off to your next class, boys," she sighed.

"What was that about, Marcus?" asked Pierce. "Yeah, were you just making it up?" asked Flipa. "No! I read it in a book, I swear. It wasn't written by the lords of Dormando, but it was in the library. I swear," said Marcus, defensively. The other boys, except Robbert, sighed. "Well, we can't just believe you," said Tippy. "Oh! Really, and why's that?" asked Marcus. "Because we'd never know if you were lying," said Tippy. "Well, I'm not lying," said Marcus. "Who knows if you just lied?" persisted Tippy. "But I didn't!" shouted Marcus. "Exactly," finished Tippy. At this point, Marcus's brain was boggled. "Pah!" he said. "What do you mean, Pah?" asked Pierce. "Never mind," said Marcus, sighing. The boys were already in the next class and Mrs. Cup was seated on her armchair.

"Welcome, boys. Please take your seats!" greeted Mrs. Cup. The boys clambered onto their highchairs. As in art classes, the tables and chairs were lean and tall. It's meant to be peaceful for the mind. "I see we have a newcomer in the class. Pierce. I am Mrs. Cup, if ye'd like to know. I hail from the village of Dormando," she said.

"Me too," replied Pierce. "Wonderful, wonderful," said Mrs. Cup, looking jolly. Mrs. Cup started scribbling something on the blackboard, when Headmaster Lyonis entered the classroom. "Hello Mrs. Cup, hello students," he said. All the boys let out a mournful 'Hello.' "Well, good morning, headmaster. We were just beginning our lesson. Any special reason you're here?" asked Mrs. Cup.

"Oh, no, no, I just wanted Marcus and Robbert to be excused for a moment, if that's possible, eh?" said the headmaster. "Oh of course! Boys, follow the headmaster will you?" said Mrs. Cup. Marcus and Robbert glanced at each other, and wondered what they had done now. They followed Headmaster Lyonis out of the class. When they were in a quiet and empty corridor, the conversation begun. "What's wrong, sir?" asked Robbert, nervously. "Ah, yes. I'm sure you both remember the gold dragon that helped you save the school last year," the headmaster said. "Oh! Yes, sir, we go and meet him every week," said Marcus. "Well, I was walking around outside the gates this morning, and he passed by. He asked me to let you know that he wants to have a little chat with the both of you," headmaster Lyonis announced. "Oh! Okay. Maybe Goldfire's teeth are in trouble with those blackberries again. We'll go meet him, but when?" asked Robbert. "Now." said the headmaster sternly. "Oh! Where, sir?" asked Marcus. "Outside the front gate," replied the headmaster. With that, the boys shrugged and wandered down the corridors, towards the main gate.

Once they arrived at the gates, the portcullis was pulled up, and they exited the school. There, they saw Goldfire, the gold dragon, perched upon one of the great graves of the lords of Dormando. He was looking quite busy, sharpening his claws on the ground, and picking his teeth. After a few moments, he noticed them. "Well, hello boys," he greeted them, gruffly. I'm sorry I had to take you away from your class," he said. "Oh, no. We're quite alright and happy. Missing class is like a dream, but better," said Marcus, happily. Goldfire snorted a puff of smoke. "So, what's going on?" Robbert asked, casually. "Are the blackberries making your teeth ache again?" he asked. "Well yes, that's always happening. They are really sour. Who knows why they're called berries, eh? More like dead flies. I wish I could lay my claws on those pesky sheep lurking around. They're always walking by me at dinner time, making me feel like grabbing them and tearing their fluffy bodies into pieces," explained Goldfire, looking over at the farms down in the village. The boys followed his gaze but weren't very surprised.

"So, that is why you called us here? To tell us about sheep?" asked Marcus, annoyed. "Oh, good heavens, I forgot to tell you both something very important!" cried Goldfire.

"Well?" said Robbert. "I have to leave," Goldfire said. The boys stared at him in confusion. "What? What do you mean 'leave'?" asked Marcus skeptically. "I haven't told you this before, but I am from Frohaven, just as all gold dragons are. I need to go back there," said Goldfire, sadly, awaiting his friends' response. "Why haven't you told us this before?" they asked. Goldfire said, "I thought you might have got afraid, so I waited a little longer until you both were a year older. Gold dragons start dying if they don't bask in the great golden lakes in Frohaven. They can survive for a couple of years, but I've been away nearly three. I could fall ill anytime. I need to heal."

"But you can't!" exclaimed Marcus. "You're the only thing that is stopping evil invaders from swarming our land. What if…" Marcus stopped himself. Things were getting intense. "I am too weak now. Evil things will come even if I am here. I cannot fight. I assure you; I will be back to protect the land as soon as I heal back," explained Goldfire. Marcus was out of words now. "Come on Robbert. We're done here," he said, turning his back on Goldfire. Robbert wanted to say something, but was afraid his friend would pick up a stone and bonk him on the head, so he simply followed Marcus back to the castle. He cast a last glance at Goldfire, guiltily.

He felt bad leaving Goldfire there. He tried to look back again, but Goldfire was gone, soaring through the sky like an eagle towards his homeland. Frohaven…

———•———

6

And the Spears Fly through the Sky (Part 2)

After four days of travel under harsh conditions, the army of the Stronghold arrived at the doorstep of Necropolis. Necropolis could just about be seen, through the mists. "At last, we are on the verge of battle. It took longer than it should have," said Kragg, standing up. "Hmmm… so it begins," muttered Rackor.

The ships circled around the island from a distance. They couldn't be seen, thankfully, or else their plan would have failed terribly. The sailors heeded the instructions well and sailed to the east side. According to the vampires, there were no watchtowers on the east, so they could sneak up on the village without sounding an alert. After an hour or so, the ships halted at the shore. Slowly, the army of the Stronghold emerged. The goblins came first, then the bigger creatures. Kragg cleared his throat, as he got ready to give the army a pep talk. He loved giving speeches. "It's for the greater good," he said. The carriage that Kragg and the vampires were in rocked a bit as Kragg called for everyone's attention. "Ahem… to all of the army!" he boomed. "It is with great honor that I present to you the land of Necropolis," he said turning his gaze ahead.

"Har! Har! Hee-hee, Ha hah!" the army broke into laughter as Necropolis was a bit different and, you could say 'puny'. "What are they laughing about?" asked Rackor, menacingly. "Oh, they've never seen Necropolis like this before, terribly sorry… calm yourselves fellow goblins and others! Yes, not what you expected, but it is what it is. Nothing to say. We are here for one reason only!" Kragg said looking upon his faithful army. "To wreak havoc and get these vampires their revenge!" The vampires stood up so everyone in the army could see them.

"One of our goblins will launch a spear when I give the order, to tell our foes what's coming. Good luck, my children, good luck," Kragg finished, as he slumped back to his throne. "Hooray!" the army cheered and marched on.

Pwaaaaa, the horn sounded.

6

And the Spears Fly through the Sky (Part 3)

Marcus, Robbert and the other students headed to the last class for the day. Self- defense. "Hello students," said Mr. Vlad. "I hope you remember what we did in last class, with the weapons?" he asked. "Yes, Mr. Vlad!" the boys said in unison. "Wonderful, wonderful. I think I mentioned we would discuss the legends of Dormando. I hope you all have gathered some information?" he asked. The students nodded to say they had. "Okay. We won't be doing any activity today, so there's no need to get up. Marcus snorted. He still was mad at Goldfire. "Do you know the names of the greatest fighters? I'm expecting the famous ones will be known," said Vlad. Some of the boys raised their hands. "Hmmm, Flipa?" asked Vlad. "Yes sir, I know Sir Dormando the courageous. Very famous indeed," answered Flipa proudly. "Yes! He is the most important person. Sir Dormando, the greatest knight. Five-hundred years ago he fought in the great army. Oh! What great things he did. The land was named after him when he died," explained Mr. Vlad. All the students nodded proudly. "Now, who knows Victor Bullseye, eh?" asked Mr. Vlad. "Ooh! Ooh!" cried Malop, and he raised his hand. None of the other boys knew Victor Bullseye. "Go ahead boy, tell us," said Vlad. "Malop's the name sir. Victor Bullseye was the greatest archer ever!

His name is recorded as the best bowman ever!" said Malop. He was so excited that he told Mr. Vlad he might switch to bows. "Precisely, Malop. We'll think about it, but great detail you have given us."

As the class continued, the sky suddenly went dark. The boys found it very odd for a time like this. Then, it started drizzling...

It had not rained for months! Why was it happening now? "Why in the devil's pits is it dark?! It's not even afternoon!" exclaimed Mr. Vlad. "Well, this is not good. Class dismissed," continued Vlad as he wiped the water trickling down the side of his head. "Hurry on inside the castle now," he instructed to the boys. The students walked briskly towards the castle. Vlad gathered his books and hurried along with the boys. He squinted at the sky. It was all very odd. Then, something caught his eye. The group walked silently for a while. Vlad was looking skyward when he spotted a large stick falling through the sky. "Pffftttt! Just a twig or something. Ha-ha... Someone would have thought..." Vlad murmured but then his eyes felt like they were going to pop out of their very sockets!

"Spear!" he yelled. A large pointy spear was soaring in the direction of the boys and Vlad. The boys were confused and turned around to see Vlad. Vlad quickly shoved them to the ground along with himself. "Mr. Vlad! What's wrong? Cough! Cough!" asked Malop tumbling over. Moments later, a spear landed next to them. It buried itself in the ground, piercing the dirt. No one spoke as the boys got up with Mr. Vlad. Vlad picked up the spear observantly. "S-sir...," whimpered Mar. "W-what... Where d-did that c-come f-from?" asked Robbert looking terrified. "Boys, I do not know, but something is heading our way. Something nasty. We need to warn the headmaster! Run for the castle! Make sure you conceal yourselves when you get there. I'll be right behind you…," said Mr. Vlad.

The boys charged down the path like a pack of gazelles. Vlad was behind them, he grabbed his sword from his scabbard. What was coming? What was heading for the castle?

7

The Army of the Stronghold

The army could see the village of Dormando very clearly now. "We are at battle! Blow the horn!" ordered Kragg. Pwaaaaa, the horn sounded once more. People from the village rushed out of their houses and huts to see what was going on. Tower men were scouting the area suspiciously. And then, the army revealed itself. Hundreds of monsters. The villagers froze with fear. The feared Army of the Stronghold had arrived…

* * *

The students rushed into the castle, followed by Vlad, and shut the gates. "Phew!" sighed the boys. Drenched because of the rain, they headed straight to the changing rooms to dry themselves. In the meanwhile, Headmaster Lyonis arrived with a few other boys. "Ah! Mr. Vlad! How wonderful, we thought you were still outside in the rain. I see the boys are all dry now," said the headmaster. "Mr. Headmaster! We had to rush in to warn you all! Something destructive is heading this way!" exclaimed Vlad, walking around in terror. "I don't understand! What is the meaning of this?" asked the headmaster, confused.

"We were on our way back to the castle, when a spear landed next to us! It was a warning! We need to secure the castle," explained Vlad. The headmaster was stunned.

"We must escort all of the children to the hall! Make an announcement we must!" cried Headmaster Lyonis. "Quickly, you boys, along with Biscuit and Finny, go to the main hall. Vlad, you must find as many swordsmen as you can and get them ready for battle!" instructed Headmaster Lyonis. "Yes, sir," agreed Vlad. "Wait for the other boys and teachers… they will join you shortly," said the headmaster to the students.

"What do you think is happening?" Robbert asked Marcus. "I don't know, but it's something big," he said. The group awaited the other forty-two students. No longer than five minutes had passed and the forty-two students filled the hall with Dram the janitor, Mrs. Bertus and Mrs. Cup ushering them in like a bunch of bamboozled baboons. "Come now, no need to panic! Settle down! The other boys are here too," explained Mrs. Bertus. She sighed as the students began to chat. "What's going on?" a student cried out from somewhere. "Yeah! Tell us! We have the right to know," said another. "Well… sigh… it seems like some sort of green, brown and white army has infested the lower Dormandian village and is causing havoc!" said Mrs. Bertus warily. Everyone gasped at this horrifying news. A few even screamed.

"Wait!" called Marcus suddenly, as he figured out what had happened. "There is only one army of the sort! Vast monstrous creatures from the land of Karabor!" he continued, stepping up onto the teacher's podium so that everyone could see him clearly. "Hey, it's that Marcus fellow," a few murmured. "Yeah!" others whispered. "Marcus Arthur Fedrick, what the dickens is happening?" a voice boomed. All the boys gasped and cleared the path to Marcus, revealing Headmaster Lyonis behind them. Marcus looked to the right, then the left. "Sir, I wanted to tell everyone about the… goblins," said Marcus. "I see, you are expecting the arrival of the army of the Stronghold?" asked Headmaster Lyonis worried. Marcus and Robbert both wondered how the old headmaster knew about the army of the Stronghold…

"Y-yes," said Marcus. "Ah! I believe you," said the headmaster, adding, "You shall lead us to safety, as you seem to have good knowledge about these… creatures. Your friend, Robbert Algar Fedrick, shall help you. Come our faithful saviors! Do what is right and lead us to safety," announced the headmaster. Marcus nodded, and Robbert nudged him. "You have a plan? It's a sticky situation out there." he asked. "Yup, just a moment," Marcus replied. They looked around the hall, scanning everyone's faces. "Well, everyone evacuate to the dungeon! Last one there will probably most certainly become goblin food," announced Marcus. He rushed down the hall with Robbert, barging through the doors and heading towards the trapdoor. "Very well," sighed Headmaster Lyonis as he led the pupils to the dungeon.

* * *

Vlad, the self-defense teacher, trudged out of the castle. He saw that the sky was now pitch black and it was raining very heavily. "Oh! Boy…" he huffed when a lightning bolt struck the fields, starting a small flame. Vlad charged down the cobbled path to Dormando village.

He was very concerned about the villagers, as they had not been prepared for such a mysterious ambush from nowhere. As he got closer, he heard the screaming and the destruction that was taking place…

Vlad jogged up to the top of a grassy hill that gave him a good view of the village.

"Goblins," said Vlad. Then he saw some ape-like creatures, covered in snow-like fur. He couldn't see them clearly, but he knew that village of Dormando was about to meet its end.

Vlad sprinted a long distance to the barracks. He thought he could round up a small army of swordsmen and, hopefully slow the goblins of their evil deeds. But as he entered, he saw blood splattered all over the floor. "This is not good; blood of innocent souls has been spilt on this dark day…" Vlad muttered. One helpless soldier was dead. It looked like he had been struck with a blade and then violently bitten on the neck. "Eh… terrible…" said Vlad, sorrowfully, waging through the mucky floor. Suddenly, a goblin scurried down the stairs to the swords room. It noticed Vlad immediately and leaped at him, blade in hand. Vlad reacted quickly, he drew his sword and bashed the goblin hard on its head. It fell dead on the floor. Greenish-brown blood dripped from the monster's large ears. Vlad ran up the stairs looking for survivors of this ruthless attack on the barracks. There were none. There was no time to linger, so Vlad said his prayers and charged out of the barracks hurriedly. He charged down the road to the village. "Yeah! For the swordsmen of Dormando!" Vlad cried as he leapt over the fences and grass.

Amidst all the mayhem, an enormous ogre spotted Vlad and started stomping towards him like a bull after a red flag. Vlad smiled, and then drew his sword. Before the ogre could act, Vlad got behind it and jumped upon the ogre's greasy back. "Arghhh! Grawww!" the irritated ogre moaned as it tried to shake Vlad off its back. There was enough time for Vlad to steadily bury his sword into the great beast's enormous back.

It took a few moments, but the ogre lost its senses and started to lose its body too. Vlad leaped off the ogre, as it plummeted to the ground. "Phew!" exhaled Vlad as he took a moment to regain his balance.

* * *

As Vlad approached the village, he spotted a couple of goblins trying to break into a village house. Through the window, he could see a helpless child seated on the floor, crying, for his parents had not returned after they had left for bringing groceries. Vlad was too astonished to speak. He got his blade ready and rushed at the goblins, taking them by surprise. "Eh?" said one of the goblins as Vlad chopped their heads off at once. They tumbled to the ground. "Foolish creatures," thought Vlad as he entered the house.

The crying boy glanced at Vlad and got scared. "P-please don't h-hurt m-me," he spluttered. "No, no. I'm here to help you," said Vlad as he shut the door.

He helped the boy stand up. Then, he took him to the back of the house. The child was shivering with fear. Vlad found a small attic. They climbed the ladder and he asked the child to stay there. "Stay here in the attic. You will be safe here, I promise. Do not leave," instructed Vlad. The child stared at him, whimpering. Vlad climbed down the ladder then cut it up. He made sure the goblins would not be able to reach the child easily. "I am going now. I will try to save the others," said Vlad and exited the house quickly.

In the village, he started taking out the goblins one by one. "Yeah! Urgh!" Vlad sank his sword inside a goblin's back. "Screech!" He stopped running to catch his breath when… he saw a huge creature.

"Holy devils… a behemoth!" said Vlad to himself. As he retreated to save himself, the behemoth spotted Vlad. He charged at Vlad, but Vlad pounced onto a pile of hay, narrowly missing the behemoth's blood-curdling claws. He swiftly got back on his feet and gripped his sword tightly. The enormous creature swiped its clutching claws at Vlad. They barely missed him, as he jumped onto the beast's back! "Yarrrr!" he grunted, struggling to cling on. The behemoth tried to come to its senses and then started shaking its body manically, trying to get Vlad to pass out or fall off. Vlad managed to somehow climb the beast's back. After a minute, he was able to see the head of the behemoth. He was about to chop it off, but suddenly, crack! A goblin archer from nowhere shot an arrow right into Vlad's arm, injuring him badly. Blood streamed out of his arm. Vlad yelped, and was too weak to hold his weapon anymore. He dropped it and rolled off the behemoth's hide, tumbling to the ground in agony. He tried to stand up, but his legs wouldn't hold. He collapsed into the stack of hay next to him. His back was broken and he was in too much pain to do anything. The last thing he saw was the behemoth destroying a village house, the same one he left that child in… After that, everything was a blur. Vlad was not dead, but he felt like he was. He lay in the hay, blood swallowing up his arm…

* * *

"Next time, you need to keep a sharper eye on the behemoths!" scolded Kragg, menacingly. Kragg and the vampires were still seated in the grand carriage, at quite a safe distance from the destruction. Two of the commander goblins, Ivy and Crooked were speaking with Kragg about Vlad. "There is no way to stop those blood-thirsty beasts, sire! We will send fifteen goblins for each behemoth. They can hopefully keep a watch on the savages, though I do not think we'd be seeing too much of heroics from the villagers much more sire." argued Crooked. "Very well. But, even if one behemoth falls, oh no…" paused Kragg, "I'll have you both thrown into the arena when get back to the stronghold," he warned. The goblins quickly jumped out of the carriage, and charged back into the village with their torches to order the other creatures to keep watch on the behemoths.

* * *

All the students were hurrying for the dungeon's trapdoor. Marcus, Robbert and Headmaster Lyonis were leading them to the secret entrance in the castle, which was hidden near the main gate. "Hurry on now, keep moving everyone! Come!" called the headmaster, barging into the dungeon. He was followed by Marcus, Robbert and the rest of the students. Once everyone was inside the dungeon, Headmaster Lyonis told the teachers to lock all the openings and trapdoors that they could find. They did as they were told, and the students dragged a few chairs and tables and stacked them around in front of the main trapdoor for extra safety. The crowd cleared a little bit to the sides so Marcus, Robbert and the headmaster were reasonably noticeable. Yes, the dungeon was a bit small for fifty and almost definitely more people. Then, the headmaster got ready with an important order, "No one will leave the dungeon from now on! Am I clear?" he instructed. All heads nodded. "Good! Marcus, Robbert? What is your plan for us?" he asked.

All eyes turned to them while Marcus stopped a moment to think. Robbert didn't have a clue what was going on in Marcus's mind, so he just stared at Marcus trying to read his thoughts. "Well, we all need to be very quiet and listen. I cannot predict what is going to happen unless we hear sounds and vibrations. They will give us the answers of what we must do further," said Marcus.

Headmaster Lyonis wasn't the only one with a confused look on his face. "Marcus is right! Once we hear the monsters, we can plan accordingly," said Robbert. "They are right. I see now. Everyone be still and quiet," whispered Mr. Man to everyone. Then, the dungeon went silent as if no one was there.

Kragg was impressed. The havoc his army caused was sinister. Now it was time to go for the castle. Kragg looked out of the carriage, where a few goblin guards and scouts stood waiting for further orders. "Ah, Woden my fellow! Blow the horn, will yeh? It's time for the castle to crumble," called Kragg. The guard picked up his horn and blew, Pwaaaaa! This was a signal to all the creatures. Goblins stopped torching huts, behemoths put down trees, ogres stopped stomping on people and cyclops stopped throwing boulders at big groups of cottages. Kragg stood up and picked up his horn. He spoke into it, "To the army! It is time! The castle must fall! They are under siege! We will destroy the castle, and we will pick up a handful of children and teachers! Then, we shall move out! Back to the boats then! And we will be on our way home to Karabor!" All cheered. "Onward my pets!" he bellowed, as he took a seat. "Yarrrr!" roared the army as they marched towards the castle. The land of new Dormando was doomed… THE END WAS NIGH!

* * *

Marcus heard it. He heard a loud, scary voice speak. "Did anyone else here that?" asked Marcus. Many hands shot up. The headmaster, teachers and Robbert nodded as well. Marcus guessed it was the voice of the supposedly great ruler, Kragg. "I know that voice. It was the ruler Lord Kragg. Ruler of Karabor. A lord of part of our world itself, more likely…" explained Marcus. Many faces were blank, others looked horrified. "In a few moments, our castle will start to fall. I have no idea what we shall do!" cried Marcus sorrowfully. The army was on their doorstep! Crash!!! A huge boulder crashed into one of the castle's turrets. "Everyone, be calm now!" the headmaster said, gravely. Even he did not know what was going to occur now, despite being the head of the school which is basically his job, knowing what to do and telling everyone else to do it…

Crash!!! Another boulder crashed right into the main hall. It was looking hopeless now. Crash!!! One more destroyed the gates and entrance to the castle. Goblins were marching towards the gates. "Good lord, save our precious castle," prayed the headmaster. Marcus could not take this anymore. He didn't want to be stuck, sitting like a duck in an old dusty dungeon, when he could be killing monsters instead. He walked up to Robbert and whispered something in his ear. "Everyone in Robbert's and my dorm, stand with me here, please," Marcus cried. Flipa, Scabber, Mar, Malop, Prith, Pierce and Tippy emerged from the crowd. Robbert whispered Marcus's plan to the other seven. "But why us?" asked Malop.

"You are the only ones we can trust, right now," said Marcus softly. The seven nodded. This was brave of Marcus. A dangerous plan, but brave.

"Go…" he whispered, signaling to the others. Marcus, Robbert and the seven students grabbed any weapons they could find in the dungeon. "What are you doing?!" called the headmaster, confused.

The boys pushed aside the tables and chairs and burst through the trapdoor, pushing it open with their weapons. "Stop this instant!" ordered Lyonis, but the boys did not stop to listen. They started charging up the stairs that led to the main gates.

Headmaster Lyonis had no choice but to chase them down. A couple of teachers tried to follow too but couldn't keep up. Goblins started to swarm into the castle, almost at the very same time.

"Oh Children! Where are youuu?" croaked a terrible voice. Marcus gasped along with the others. The boys hurried to the main hall and saw hordes of goblins approaching, ready to pounce on them. Marcus was terrified on the inside, but it was the right thing to lead the group and stand up for his home. Headmaster Lyonis couldn't catch the boys either because he was stiff with fear whistling through his mind. "Yarrrr!" Marcus roared as he jumped on the goblins. "Yeah! Let me at 'em!" cried Robbert. The rest of the boys drew their weapons as well. The headmaster snarled, and then walked over to the wall and picked up an ancient sword which was actually for show. "Heh," he chuckled as he swung the sword and gripped it tight. The goblins were in awe and a bit frightened as well because they could not see how many children were there with their weapons. Marcus noticed this advantage and asked the others to form a line so that the monsters could not see farther. Then, he threw his sword around maniacally, killing goblins everywhere. Robbert was at it too, sticking his giant axe into many heads. The others boys followed them, bows and spears in hands. The boys fought hard and made their way through the many numbers of the goblins and got out the castle gate…

They could not believe what they were seeing. An army so big, it could take out hundreds of towns, not just one. They saw many, many berserk creatures. Ogres, huge armored animals, trolls, legions of goblins, humongous ape-like monsters, and carriages as well. One of them was bigger than the rest. Marcus guessed it carried the ruler Kragg. "Those children! That teacher! Capture them, for the devil's sake!" yelled a goblin. "Yeah! Kragg's orders!" chipped in another, but Marcus was in no mood to give up. "I am very sorry my boys…" said Headmaster Lyonis. The children suddenly realized he was by their side. "But there is nothing we can do now," he said. Marcus denied him and charged at the army of creatures. The others followed, while the headmaster tried to keep up, not able to convince the boys. They were upon the goblins, when a huge ape-like creature stepped forward. It flung its claws around, sending Marcus and Robbert flying. "Behemoth!" cried the headmaster, as he took a step back. The other seven froze in terror. The behemoth swept some goblins away like they were cockroaches. Now, the students and Headmaster Lyonis were surrounded, with no escape. In the meantime, Marcus crashed into a tree, while Robbert went plummeting into a huge boulder.

"Joy! We have completed our mission! Holy devils! Now, fire at the castle!" yelled Kragg. Cyclops received the orders, and resumed flinging boulders at the castle, smashing different parts of the structure.

Marcus was in great pain. His leg was broken, surely. He managed to get a glimpse of the havoc. The castle was almost completely reduced to a pile of rubble. Luckily, the dungeon was underground, away from the army's sight. Stones crumbled and glasses shattered. Marcus spotted Robbert resting on a rock. He was badly knocked out. Marcus's eyes hurt, and so they closed…

Within moments, the army was ready to travel back to Karabor, their task accomplished. The remaining seven boys and their headmaster were thrown into a cage, which was carried by an ogre. The entire army emerged from the mainland and reached the coast of Necropolis, where all the ships were docked, in perfect order. They settled into the vessels and placed the cage with the prisoners in the lower deck of one of the vessels. Once all the creatures were onboard, they set sail for Karabor, leaving behind a newly brought-up town in ruins…

Part 2

The Journey Through the Mountains

8

Mrs. Groom's Healing Home

Marcus blinked. He was lying down on a small bed. He looked around. He was surprised to see the school's new teacher, Vlad, lying on a bed at the other end of the room. His eyes were shut, and it looked like he was sleeping. Marcus wondered how he got hurt and if sir Vlad was alright. The only thing he remembered from that forsaken day was the sensation of being smashed into a tree. The Army of the Stronghold was gone… Marcus tried to lift himself off the bed, but something restrained him. A sharp pain shot through his legs, which sent him flopping back onto the bed. Then, he saw a bunch of bandages and clothing wrapped around his whole leg. He realized that he was injured, and grazed his leg terribly and it was very serious. "Argh!" he screamed in pain. Just then, a few familiar faces burst through the door. One person, however, was unrecognizable. It was Mrs. Bertus, Mr. Dickens, and a short lady who he had never met before. "A very good afternoon to you, Marcus," said Mr. Dickens. "H-hello…" said Marcus, weakly. "The boy needs rest," the short lady said. "What h-happened?" asked Marcus. "Well, after that wretched army left our land in rubble, we found you lying next to a tree! The village was very unstable, but we were able to carry you to this small healing home, which is run by this lady, Mrs. Groom" explained Mrs. Bertus pointing at a short lady. Then, Mrs. Groom spoke, "Well, Mr. Marcus, you are very lucky your injury wasn't too severe and I was able to heal you quickly. After a couple of days, today is your last day here. You should be fit and good to go by 7 o' clock at the latest." "Great. Thank you." said Marcus.

"But where is Robbert, Mr. Dickens? Is he alright?" asked Marcus. "Oh yes! Robbert is completely fine. A few bruises and gashes here and there, but he is fine. Mrs. Groom did give him a little bit of rest, however," said Mr. Dickens. "In fact, he's sitting outside in the waiting room right now. We were waiting there as well, until we heard you yelp," added Mrs. Bertus. "C-can I see him?" asked Marcus. "Well, maybe later Marcus. He's a bit groggy right now," answered Mr. Dickens. Marcus chuckled to himself. "If you'd like to know, most of the students have been returned to their families. Some, who lost their parents due to the attack, have been escorted to Mrs. Stool, the local nanny and matron of the Rabbitling orphanage," explained Mr. Dickens, sadly. Marcus hung his head low. "A lot of houses were also destroyed in the attack, though most inns have been safe for taking refuge. Families who lost their huts, have been given free space in the inns until they can build new homes. Those who still have their houses, remain in peace. You'll be glad to know that Robbert's home did not get destroyed, so you won't have to be living at an inn," said Mrs. Bertus. "But-but… what about Malop, Prith, Scabber, Mar, Pierce, Tippy, Flipa and headmaster Lyonis? We can't leave them to die at the hands of those filthy goblins! The monsters will have them for supper! We have to rescue them!" exclaimed Marcus.

The two teachers looked at each other and then at Marcus. Then, Mr. Dickens said, "I am terribly sorry Marcus, but there is really nothing we can do. Firstly, we lost all our soldiers in the battle. There is no way we can step into a war. You saw the beasts. We are nothing compared to them. And secondly, we don't even know where those goblins are! They could be on the other end of the world, or they could be at the bottom of the sea, or even inside a mountain!" Marcus pleaded, "But we have to try." Mr. Dickens continued, "I know, but we can't risk more lives. We are risking the whole population of Dormando.

I promise, we will have a mourning or a gathering. That's that!" Marcus wasn't going to let that happen. "The boy is right…," said a familiar voice. The group turned to see Vlad staring into space. "Sir!" cried Marcus. "Oh! Thank heavens the fellow is alive!" cried Mrs. Bertus with her hands on her head.

"Even though my legs, arms and back are broken, I am with the child," the fearless man gestured. Marcus saw many casts on Vlad's body. "Oh! He's in more trouble than you are, Mr. Marcus. He had a painful night. Four dozes of healing liquid were given to him until he fell asleep!" explained Mrs. Groom looking over at Vlad, giving him a nasty look. "You devil of a lady! Witch!" cursed Vlad as he struggled to move.

"Take it easy you fool, or I'll have to give you more doses! What were you thinking? Climbing something a hundred times bigger than you, and the worst of it- falling off! Put me in real pain you did!" yelled Mrs. Groom. "Why you…" faltered Vlad. He muttered his curses to himself. "Well, Marcus, it is almost dusk. We will retrieve you in three hours and then drop you off at the Fedrick's'," said Mrs. Bertus. Marcus nodded off as the two teachers left the room.

9

To the Pile of Rubble

It was 4 o' clock in the morning. Marcus was awake. Last night, he left Mrs. Groom's hospital, and was now at Robbert's house. It was just turning dark when he arrived at Robbert's, so he went straight to bed. No dinner, no wash and not even any questions. He was really tired even though he had been sleeping for the last three days. Marcus sat up in his bed. His leg didn't hurt much anymore, it was just a bit sore. He stepped out of his room for a glass of water when he saw Robbert. "I knew you'd be awake," said a sleepy Robbert. "Is your leg much better?" "Fine, really," replied Marcus. "Good then. I wonder how the castle looks, now that it's been destroyed," said Robbert. Then, Marcus got an idea. "So why don't we go look around? No one's awake right now, right?"

"No, it probably should be okay to go at this hour. That's a great idea," agreed Robbert.

The two boys went back to their rooms and changed into their old clothes, as they couldn't possibly go out in a night dress. It was cold and cloudy and very quiet. It looked like dawn would soon break.

"Maybe we shouldn't go at this time. It looks so hollow out there," said Robbert, warily. "Oh come now, it's only a bit damp, nothing more," said Marcus.

"Okay, okay…," said Robbert. He was still shook by the army of the stronghold's destruction. The two of them walked down a path that led out of the village to the castle. "Revolting!" groaned Robbert as he smelt blood and bones everywhere he went. After about fifteen minutes of walking, they were on the hill where the castle stood. It was completely destroyed.

The only thing standing was a broken turret, which looked like it could topple over any moment. The boys approached the castle carefully. "We have to be quiet and cautious. Any loud sound could cause an avalanche from those standing towers," said Marcus, softly. "Okay, but, by Merlin's beard, those boulders are really big," said Robbert, now that he was actually close up to one. "Look at it. It can kill a dragon!" cried Robbert a little loudly. Now, Robbert imagining things. "Quieter. I beg to differ though, Robbert," said Marcus, looking at Robbert funny. "Okay, okay. Maybe you need a bigger boulder…" said Robbert, realizing the unrealistic thing he had stated.

The two boys waded through the rubble, until they came across an unmistakable, perfectly in shape, trapdoor. "The dungeon!" they both cried together.

10

Fiddlin

"Should we be going down there?" asked Robbert. "I'm not so sure," replied Marcus. He wondered if anyone was in there. Then, they heard an unfamiliar voice. "Oy! Yeh stupid rodents! Gerroff me grub!" yelled a grouchy voice. The boys' eyes widened. "Someone is in there," whispered Marcus. "Maybe someone was left behind when everyone exited the dungeon. Let's help them out," replied Robbert. "Alright, but stay on guard…" said Marcus, doubtful. The boys slowly lifted the trapdoor. It creaked quietly. Then the voice spoke, "Now, it's about time I get meself a rabbit. I been livin' of these crumbs for far too long!" The boys treaded carefully down the staircase. Marcus felt uneasy, his thoughts racing. He wondered if whoever was down there was human or not. "Or maybe a whole cow…" continued the voice cackling, but fell silent when Marcus asked, "Hello?" There was no reply, and a cold sensation crawled up the boys' spines. Marcus was next to a table with weapons. He picked up an old spear, just in case. Robbert grabbed an axe. That terrible voice surely did not belong to any mere human.

Then, suddenly, a creature leaped at them. "Raaaar!" cried the thing, while trying to pin the boys to the ground. "Ow! Get off of me, villain!" cried Robbert as he kicked the monster away. Next thing they knew, the boys were looking at a green, hairy face. "Children?! What the buttock are yeh doin' down 'ere?" hissed the familiar figure.

Marcus realized that this was a goblin. "I could ask you the same!" yelled Marcus. "I asked first!" demanded the goblin.

"Wait, aren't you going to slay us and have us for breakfast?" wondered Robbert. "Well, you seem like you want me to! Should I, hmm?" asked the goblin menacingly. "Please don't! Heh heh, I was just wondering…" begged Robbert.

"Besides, I already had me breakfast and I never really had a taste for yeh kind. I'm the gentlest goblin there is! I'm the goblin who refused to slay the other goblin to become a commodore! That makes me good for me kind, eh!" explained the goblin. The boys were really confused. "Throttling us didn't seem very gentle," said Robbert. "You were the ones who surprised me, you great oafs!" denied Fiddlin. "Yeah, well we are the children from the school your army destroyed. I'm Marcus and he's Robbert, got it?" ordered Marcus. "Yeah, yeah. Really, are those yer names? Never heard names like them. M'names Fiddlin. I was forced to help in destroying your village and castle," he said. "Well, Mr. Fiddlin, why are you down here, when your army is sailing away to another land?" asked Robbert. "Well, when us goblins broke into the castle, you fellows came out and started slaying us. I ran over to a bog and shut meself in! I was in the front anyway, and I didn't want to be killed. Later, I saw all of yer folk getting out of this trapdoor thingy, long after me brothers had left.

After I was sure all of yeh had left, I decided to open the old john and hide elsewhere. I opened this trapdoor to find this perfect hideout, full of weapons. Thought I'd survive unnoticed until I die 'ere. Guess not now, eh," explained Fiddlin. Marcus and Robbert understood Fiddlin. Marcus thought of asking Fiddlin something, "Mr. Fiddlin," said Marcus, but was cut off. "Fiddlin is fine, 'choo sayin'?" asked Fiddlin crouching on the ground. "Fiddlin. I was wondering if you could tell us where our friends have been taken by your… army.?" asked Marcus. "Now, why would yeh want to know that?" questioned Fiddlin, very suspicious. "Well, we thought… we thought we could rescue our friends, but we're not sure where they are," said Marcus, giving it away. Fiddlin jumped up.

"I aren't telling yeh nothin'! I know what yer concocting, yeh thieving dogs! I'll tear you apart!" cried Fiddlin, trying to get at the boys' heels. "We'll help you! We'll help you!" spluttered Robbert as he kicked Fiddlin off once more. "Help me? Wh-why? With what?" asked Fiddlin, confused.

"You want to get back to your tribe, right? Well, we're trying to get to your tribe too, just not in a very welcoming way. We're basically aiming for the same thing, but can't do it without your guidance, because we have no idea where your homeland is. You can't leave new Dormando now. You'll be skinned before you can even get your hands on a boat! And, even if we find our friends, we'll be eaten before we can even see them! Don't you see? We both are going the same way, are we not?" explained Marcus.

The boys could see that Fiddlin was making up his mind, muttering to himself. "Well," he paused. The boys waited impatiently for a response. "That is wonderous! I can go home, and on the way, I can repay you with help to get there! Hurrah!" cried Fiddlin. The boys sighed in content. "Well, Fiddlin, where do we go?" asked Marcus grinning. "Oh yes, Karabor. The Stronghold," said Fiddlin, still leaping around. The boys froze like ice-cubes. "Oh! C'mon. It aren't much of a journey!" said Fiddlin, but suddenly his grin turned into a frown. "Wait a minute, why do yeh want to get to Karabor again?

Get revenge on me brothers, do yeh?" asked Fiddlin, threateningly. "Well, because our friends are just kids like us, we can't leave them to be killed. And your friends or brothers forgot all about you and left you here," said Marcus, rather convincingly. Fiddlin thought for a minute. "Of course. Now I understand that you are right! Those savages, leaving me behind. I'll 'git em!" yelled Fiddlin.

"So, erm, Fiddlin. When are going to leave from here?" asked Robbert. "Now, of course!" cried Fiddlin. "Now?! We haven't even packed supplies!" replied Marcus.

"Fine, I'll give yeh an hour. Suppose we can't leave without food and gear, eh." agreed Fiddlin. He told the boys that he was also going to get the weapons ready. With that, the boys headed home to pack and stock up for an adventure.

11

A Map and a Ship

At around half past five, Marcus and Robbert headed back to the dungeon to meet Fiddlin. They were carrying large sacks stuffed with water, food, extra clothing, some tools, and a couple of blankets for the journey to Karabor, just in case. When they entered the trapdoor, they were greeted by Fiddlin who looked quite prepared in protective clothing. "Hello lads! It is time! But first, pick your weapons," he said to them.

The boys had completely forgotten about weapons!

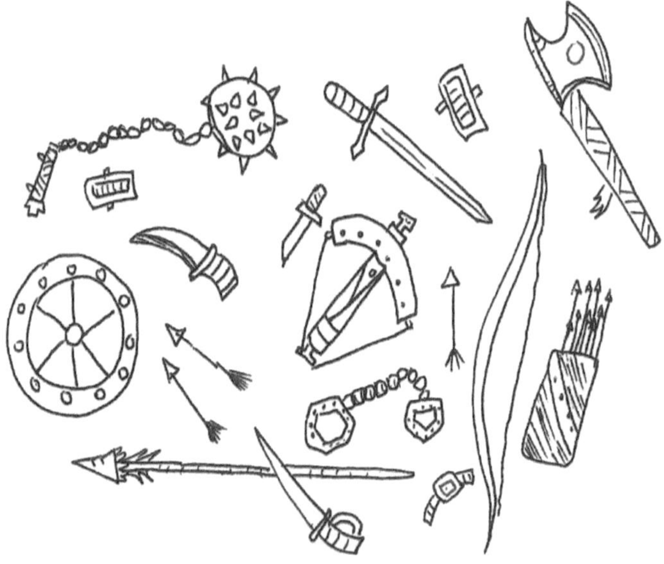

Fiddlin was armed with a set of daggers, a knife, a crossbow, and a short flail.

Marcus opted for a sword, a cutlass, a shield, a bow, and a stack of arrows in a quiver. Robbert, on the other hand, armed himself with a short sword, an axe, a pair of shackles, a shield, and a glaive his size. Fiddlin also gave them arm gauntlets and knee protectors for climbing mountains, besides a piece of torn clothing to wrap around their necks to keep them warm on the journey across the seas. They all carried a collection of small bits and bobs they needed that were attached to a sash that hung across their chests. When they stood together, they looked like they were ready to take on a dragon!

They couldn't carry all their weapons at once, so they stuffed a few of them into the rucksacks. Then, Fiddlin said, "At last, we are ready. Now it's time teh' get goin. Here it be," said Fiddlin, as he pulled out a map from his pouch. "This is the map of Arabon. The whole world really," he explained. "Woah!" exclaimed the boys excitedly. The map was truly fascinating, as it marked the areas of their world. "Now, here's where we are, Necropolis, at the top right corner.

On the left bottom is Karabor, so we ought to get to bottom right side and then set sail," explained Fiddlin "Oh! Yes! So we're taking a ship. But how are we going to get one?" asked Marcus, confused. "Yes, comin' to that, we steal a medium-sized ship, and sail onwards," said Fiddlin.

"Steal?" asked Robbert, shocked. He hoped that they didn't have to steal anything. "Are you with the plan or not, eh?" asked Fiddlin, visibly annoyed. "Okay, alright…" sighed Robbert. "From there, we sail straight ahead. Since we aren't carrying much weight, we will reach Karabor in about two days," explained Fiddlin, looking at the map. "Two days?! Will our friends have that much time?" asked

Marcus. "Well, we are sailing full speed to the other end of the world. You can't swim, and there isn't no other way to get there. Unless you have a dragon or summat, which we do not." said Fiddlin, hands akimbo. "Now, let's git' teh' the shipyard before yeh' village starts wakin' up," he added. The boys and the goblin exited the dungeon quickly, and headed for the shore. Robbert was worried about what his friends and teachers would think. Marcus too. They were not keen on stealing, though it had to be done for the greater good. There was no chance of borrowing one, as no one would believe two children and a goblin for that matter.

They had to keep Fiddlin hidden as well, because people would go berserk if they saw a goblin walking their streets. "Keep low, Fiddlin. People aren't used to seeing goblins walking down the streets," said Robbert. "Right yeh are," replied Fiddlin. Once the three of them entered the village, they became silent. No one was likely to wake up this early, except the forgers and smelters, who have been taking their jobs very seriously these days. Fiddlin lowered his head and put the piece of clothing on his neck over his head to cover his ears. They made their way through the village, until they were stopped by two big dogs clenching their teeth and growling.

"Oh! No! These are the guardsman's hounds. They've been taking extra precaution after the big siege," said Robbert, worriedly. It was Fiddlin the dogs were sniffing at. Then, suddenly, Fiddlin pulled a bone out of his pocket and threw it at the dogs. "Get it, yeh mangy mutts!" he yelled, and the dogs charged at the bone, clawing at each other. "That'll keep em off," said Fiddlin. "Whoa, who would have thought a tiny bone could stop the guardsman's hounds," said Robbert in awe. "I always keep bones handy. You never know what you might encounter, though I was saving em for bigger things. Like renocentamins…" explained Fiddlin, calmly. "What's a renocentamin?" asked Marcus. "Oh, you know! The big meat-eating horned animals in the Stronghold's army," said Fiddlin. "Ah! Very subtle," said Marcus. "Anyway, doggies aren't a big deal for me. I learnt how to deal with them during wolf riding sessions at the Stronghold," said Fiddlin, proudly. The boys looked at him, confused. The three of them reached the shipyard after a few moments.

There was an old man at a table, but he was asleep. "Alright, that's Mr. Bucket the sailor. He runs the place, so keep quiet and follow me around," whispered Marcus.

They looked around the columns, until they spotted a medium sized ship with a large sail. It looked easier to handle, unlike the huge battle ships that needed a crew. Marcus, Robbert and Fiddlin were more of a… band of warriors, you could say. "Here we are, the… Barrel Rider. Funny name, eh," said Marcus chuckling.

Robbert started chuckling too, but Fiddlin just stood there staring at the ship. The ship had a large sail and mast, a captain's quarters, the below deck for the crew, the main deck, a wheel, a bow with a sea-creature, a crow's nest and of course the rudder. There weren't any ballistae to defend the ship, however, Fiddlin approved of the ship, and it was the right size as well. The boys and the goblin boarded the ship. Fiddlin said he had a bit of sailing experience, so he took to the wheel.

Robbert climbed up to the crow's nest, and Marcus sorted out the supplies and food they had. He was also going to try to search the ship for any extra supplies. "Let us set sail, my maties!" called Fiddlin. "Yes, captain!" said both the boys, who thought it right for Fiddlin to be captain as he was leading them to Karabor. The ship left the docks smoothly, and they were on their way to Karabor.

The last thing they heard was a loud voice, "Oy! Where do you think you're going? Come back here!" cried the voice. "Hey, that voice sounds kind of familiar. I think it is Mr. Bucket… Oh! Never mind now," said Marcus looking back at the shipyard. It was too misty to spot anything, so he just took his mind off it.

12

Prisoners in Confinement

Thud! A loud sound woke Headmaster Lyonis from his long nap. He looked around and saw that the students who had been captured along with him were still in the cage. "Students?" asked Headmaster Lyonis, wearily. "Headmaster!" they exclaimed. "Phew! We were wondering when you'd wake up. We were starting to think that you had fainted forever," added Malop. "Well, I haven't. I was simply resting. Where are we anyway?" asked the headmaster hoarsely. "We're being escorted to the Stronghold, sir. A big goblin came and told us, two hours ago. Said we're probably going to be thrown into interrogation and then be burnt at the stake! Or worse..." replied Flipa, sorrowfully.

"Oh dear." said the headmaster, shaking his head. "What is interrogation, anyway?" asked Prith. "Well, interrogation is where you are questioned about your deeds. You can't escape it, and if you fail to speak, they often give you pain, such as torture," explained Flipa. "But why did they capture us in the first place? I thought they were going to destroy everything and eat us for dinner!" wondered Malop. Everyone was wondering the same thing, so no one had an answer.

"Hold up, why are Marcus and Robbert not here?" asked Headmaster Lyonis, confused. "Sir, they were mistakenly thrown away by the big ape-thing, remember? They weren't put in the cage," said Mar. "Ah! I remember now. Pity, we might have had a chance if they were with us," said the headmaster. After a few moments of silence, two big goblins came to the chamber where the cage was.

They lifted the cage up like it was a feather and exited the chamber to walk over to a carriage that would transport the cage to the Stronghold. "Put us down, you big fiends!" bellowed the headmaster. The goblins said nothing as they were delighted to be called fiends. Cruelty was the only happiness for them. "The fools! Where are your weapons children?" the headmaster asked the boys.

"Well, sir, the goblins took our weapons before locking us up. They said something about us being sneaky," said Pierce. "Good lord! Now we're definitely done for," cried the headmaster, taking no notice of the goblins who started to look annoyed. "One more word you troglodytes, and yeh won't meet yer end very nicely, yeh hear me!" shouted one of the goblins, threateningly. The group went quiet.

Not long after, the cage was attached to a chariot. The carriage on top was replaced with the cage. A goblin sat on top of the cage and started whipping the horse, which snorted. Another goblin banged the cage a few times, which signaled the horse to galop. The horse galloped through the desert to the Stronghold. "Yar!" roared the goblin as he continued to whip the horse. "Neahh!" screeched the horse as it reared its head and galloped. "How evil," whispered Malop.

The Stronghold was in sight after fifteen minutes. "Here we are," said the goblin as he jumped off the cage and then dragged it off the chariot. "By my beard!" exclaimed the headmaster as he looked upon the Stronghold. It was mighty enormous. "Shut it!" scolded the goblin, as he lifted the cage. "How rude," whispered Malop. The goblin gave Malop the evil eye, which made him shudder. Soon, another goblin arrived to help carry the cage into the hold. Two massive trolls with clubs stood before the enormous black doors.

"Kroke dob der Krug Clubamente!" bellowed one of the goblins at the trolls. They spoke in what sounded like goblinese. "Did you understand that?" asked Mar. "No, but it seemed to be a secret word of some sort," replied the headmaster.

The gates suddenly broke open, revealing a long, grand hall with a throne at the far end. Someone was bound to be seated on it.

The goblins walked down a blood red carpet (dyed with blood), towards the throne. The boys and the headmaster looked around to get a view of where they were going to be isolated until death. The place was filled with goblins. The creatures looked frightened, but some made nasty faces.

"What species be that?" hissed one of them. "Humans, you fool," spat another. The confused goblin's expression turned into a greedy grin. The monster licked its lips. "Are they for neck-biting in the mess hall? We don't usually get these," asked the goblin. "Not to me knowledge," said the other. Two goblins, who seemed to be archers, stood atop the frame above the door ready for anything, pulled back their bows. Then, suddenly, "Well, well, well. If it isn't the humans who were captured by my army," boomed a voice too deep to be a goblin's. The boys and Headmaster Lyonis turned to the throne to see the silhouette of a tall creature seated on the throne. It looked as if he was half goblin, half ogre. The body rose from the shadows and showed itself in the light. It was Kragg, king of the Stronghold and ruler of Karabor. "Lord Kragg of Karabor. It is us, and we do not wish any harm against you. We will go back to our home with no trouble, your lordship," said the headmaster calmly. The crowd of goblins burst out laughing. "I'm afraid it's not like that here!" replied Lord Kragg, loudly, stopping the laughter. Headmaster Lyonis's face fell. "You see, a few of our Necropolis friends here told us some very interesting information about your school. Something that we did not completely understand, which involved you," started Kragg.

The council of Necropolis now emerged from the shadows, glaring at the humans. The headmaster's eyes were fixed on them. "Necropolis f-friends? But the vampires were...," said the headmaster. "Oh! yes, the ones you killed were... well, most of..." explained Kragg. "Most of them? What do yeh mean? The students finished them!" cried a confused Headmaster Lyonis who had no idea of what was going on. Kragg was silent for a moment. He opened his mouth, then shut it. "That is not relevant. The matter is, how did your students vanquish most of them vampires? What's the tale? Every single piece of information will be transferred into our knowledge whether you like it or not," he said. "Don't tell them, sir," whispered Flipa. "What was that?" demanded Kragg suspiciously.

"We will not give the information under any circumstances," said Headmaster Lyonis, stiffly. All the goblins started cackling their heads off again. Then, Kragg shouted, "You have gone too far! Take them to the interrogation chamber, Tudar! Let the doctor deal with them..." An enormous, hideous goblin, stepped towards the cage and picked it up all by himself and carried it away from the throne hall down to a small corridor, which at the end revealed an enormous trapdoor.

The goblin opened it and walked down a long spiral staircase to the torture chamber.

The seven boys and the headmaster looked extremely worried when they saw a rack, iron maiden, and the dunking stool…

13

Tales at Sea

The sun was rising, when Marcus woke up. It had been a day since he, Robbert and Fiddlin were at sea. Marcus sat up in his hammock, almost tumbling out because of all the swinging bindings. He dusted himself off and ran up to the main-deck. He saw Robbert up in the crow's nest looking around. Marcus got a little closer to talk. "Good morning, Robbert! Did you find any land?!" he called out. "Good morning! No land so far except an island with nothing really.

Though I did see some weird black figures…" replied Robbert. "Well, ahoy scallywag!" cried Fiddlin. Marcus turned around and saw Fiddlin steering the wheel. "Hello Fiddlin-er-captain. Any news?" asked Marcus. "Eh, there be no such importance, though the weather be getting a bit rough and nasty. Misty it is but hopefully there be no storms. Alas, we shall be at ease," replied Fiddlin, like a sailor. "Good, good. I was able to find some useful parts on deck. A couple of old glass pots and barrels of mead. We could use it for any merchants out at sea," suggested Marcus. "Aye, well, the closer we get to Karabor, the less ships yeh will see. These are dangerous parts. Anyway, did yeh find any grub aboard?" asked Fiddlin. "Oh yeah, I found some old codfish. We could cook the cod tonight. I also found a sack of stale bread, which we could store for the journey," replied Marcus. "Mmph! Good. Now what would yeh like to do?"

"Erm, I might go down to the quarters and study the map. Who knows, I might find something interesting," replied Marcus…

The map was quite detailed and interesting, thought Marcus. Parts of it were damp and torn. Marcus noticed several ink dots. They seemed to indicate particular places on the map.

He spotted the different mainlands. On Hell fall, he observed an enormous fortress. On Frohaven, he saw a white brick castle, which must have been the royal castle. As Necropolis still had the great black castle, Marcus figured this was an old map. Karabor had a great big keep, which Marcus guessed was the Stronghold. Then he stared at the land of the Dormando. His old homeland. He felt happy and smiled at the castle imprinted there. A loud knock on the door forced Marcus to turn away from the map. "Come in," he said and opened the door for Robbert. "Fiddlin said he'll tell us some stories about the sea, as the water is pretty steady, and the ship seems to be at normal speed," said Robbert. "Sure, I'll be there in a moment," replied Marcus keen on a story.

As Robbert closed the door, Marcus took one last glance at the map. Then, he got up and headed out to the deck. Fiddlin and Robbert were seated on barrels near the mast. Once Marcus was seated too, Fiddlin began…

"Now, the story I'll be telling yeh, be true. Really 'appened," he started. "One fine day at Karabor, me and a few goblin friends thought we'd take a ship out to sea, to fish and experience thy life.

This were at a time of peace in Karabor. Me and my friends were onboard and were ready to go. But then, one o' us named Gorick got sick. So, we left 'im and sailed out to sea. Along the way, we'd caught huge fish and saw many islands. Though after a while, we started entering dangerous deep waters. I told me crew that we should be turnin' back. It was enough, because I knew something they did not. Yeh see, many sea creatures are hostile ones. Where we were heading into the cold damp seas, any monster could arise from the depths. Serpents, kelpie, the hordes of undead, drakes and… even the famous one," paused Fiddlin.

"What is it?" asked Marcus, a cold shiver running down his spine. Fiddlin looked at them and said, "The Kraken."

"The K-kraken? I thought that was a m-myth!" Robbert chipped in. "Nay, it's as real as yourself! I've seen it with me own eyes," continued Fiddlin. Marcus and Robbert listened like two bats. "That's impossible," Marcus said. "Arrrr, it aren't! My friends didn't listen ta' me. They wanted to find more, which was the opposite of what would be required," explained Fiddlin. "Fools, they were! Fools! I couldn't convince 'em! Then, late that terrible night, huge waves started smashing against our vessel. It was odd, but I knew what was under our boat. I walked to the side of the ship, but before I reached there, I found what I was looking for. An enormous, slimy, tentacle was sticking out of the ocean, like a snake," said Fiddlin. Marcus gasped. "I ran to the below-deck to warn my friends, but it was too late. The Kraken shot it's tentacle into the ship, straight into the below-deck, destroying it completely…" Fiddlin paused sadly. "My friends were dead. I was alone. Left at sea with a ravenous beast at me heels. The Kraken could 'ave killed me in a matter of seconds." This startled the boys. "But then, I stopped standing around and got an idea!" Fiddlin jumped up in excitement. "I jumped onto the tallest mast of the ship and started climbing it by the rigging. As I climbed, quicker and quicker, the ship sank lower and lower, as the Kraken pulled it with all its might. I finally got to the crow's nest and just stood there, waiting for the ship to sink," said Fiddlin as he closed his eyes. "Moments later, the beast had dragged the ship to the seabed. Now, the only thing sticking out of the sea was the crow's nest. And I was standing on it!" yelled Fiddlin.

"Then I saw one of them tentacles rising from the water. I realized that my plan was useless when the slimy thing shot towards the crow's nest. I jumped off… nothing else to do, I swam in a hurry, as far away from the Kraken as me legs could carry me," continued Fiddlin, as he sank into his barrel. "Not long later, I found some big branches afloat nearby. I quickly clambered onto one. I watched quietly as the forsaken monster demolished me comrades' ship. Suddenly, I spotted one of the Stronghold's scout ships, rowing towards me at high speed.

"They let me into the rust-bucket and asked me what I was doing out there… said I was on a ship, when the mighty Kraken came up and destroyed it. I was to be only survivor," explained Fiddlin. "Some of 'em didn't believe me, though some said they did hear the mighty rumble from the deep. Two days later, I was back in Karabor. And from then on, I always have feared them seas. Lo the Kraken," finished Fiddlin. "Woah! That was a fantastic, but a scary story Fiddlin! It felt like I was there myself! Let's hear it for Fiddlin, right Marcus?" applauded Robbert. He turned to Marcus, but he wasn't there.

"Marcus?" asked Robbert. "Yeah? I'm over here!" Marcus called out from the side of the ship. "Erm, what are you doing over there?" asked Robbert again. "I'm just looking at the water. It's turning a little lighter and greenish," replied Marcus. "Ah! We are not far from Karabor then. It's very hot in Karabor, that's why we're in the warm waters it be. Eh! A few hours, and we should be near the shores of Karabor," answered Fiddlin. "Oh! Then we'd better be prepared!" exclaimed Robbert. "Yeah! He's righ'. Both of yeh, get your stuff packed and ready, cause, as soon as we hit land, we have to start our journey whatsoever. No gazing and snacking on loaves, in fact have a bite right now. You aren't going to get any once we'd have reached there," suggested Fiddlin. "What's the hurry anyway?" asked Marcus.

"Well, there be plenty of watchtowers around Karabor. If we wait around like ducks, we are going to get snatched by guards or something like that. And a lot of them watchtowers are on the shore. If the devil may bless us, we hopefully won't spot one immediately. Even if we do kill em, they'll have enough time to bong them big bells. Each tower has a one at the tippity top, which can be heard from not less than a hundred miles or so forth.

"Even if the Stronghold itself won't receive it, the other towers will, which will set a chain, bonging it again and again. It'll keep going until the Stronghold retrieves the signal," explained Fiddlin.

"Okay, understood. We'll keep our weapons ready, in case we meet misfortune on the road. There's a lot of places to hide in these mountainous regions," agreed Marcus and headed to the below deck to bring some tools out. Robbert went to his quarters to pack some extra material while Fiddlin looked to the wheel as they approached Karabor.

<hr>

14

Doctor Reginald Vantorturer

Headmaster Lyonis and the boys were thrown out of the cage and were tightly handcuffed. They were forced into a large cubical room, with fences and prison-like bars all around. There was a big square cut out before them, through which they could see a table of some sort. Stools were lined up inside, for prisoners while they were questioned. The big ugly goblin barred the entrance with some wood, so there was no funny business…

"Take a seat, yeh ugly frog and your tadpoles too! Wait for the doctor to arrive," the goblin ordered Lyonis. Then, Prith asked, "What doctor?" But the goblin had already left. "Oh! This is just great. Now we're going to be questioned to death by some madman," muttered Tippy sarcastically. "Probably a torturer," said Malop. "Aye," chipped in the headmaster. Everyone was quiet, waiting for the 'doctor' to arrive. Moments later, a tall, lean, and a horrifyingly sharp-nosed goblin entered the room.

Everyone guessed he was the so-called doctor. He wore a long cloak as black as night that came down to his terribly thin calves. He also wore grey knee-high boots! Those dusty old half-moon spectacles perched on the brink of his nose perfectly. It was probably the only detail that made him look like a doctor. His skin was pale, unlike most other goblins who were a mix of greenish brown.

"Well, hello! 'Tis wonderful to meet you all, hmm. You must be the prisoners, of course, heh he he…," said the goblin in a menacing tone. He sounded a lot more different from the other goblins. He spoke very fluently and no slangy words. More sinister than ruthless. "Now, let us begin," he continued. He looked annoyed as he started flipping pages of an aged file, which sat on a small lectern in front of him.

"Firstly, my name is Doctor Reginald Vantorturer," the goblin said. The name already had the boys worried. "Wait, you're a torturer, and your name includes the word torturer as well?" asked Malop, a bit confused. The doctor snarled at him. "Yes, I have a feeling I'm not going to like you all very much. Now, I have a set of simple questions for thou, forged by Lord Kragg himself. If you fail to answer them, well, we know what I'm really here for." said Reginald, as he eyed the torture implements by his side. The headmaster and the students nodded. "Good, good, now… where is this gold dragon that apparently destroyed a group of our vampire allies, including the great Lord Drador of the Necropolis?" asked the torturer slyly.

The headmaster glanced at the boys, which told them that he was going to do the talking for now. "You see, Mr. Reginald, the gold dragon coincidentally had to leave, a mere two days before this Stronghold's army arrived. Said he had to go to Frohaven for a while, stay in his cave and bathe in gold. The fact is, gold makes him stronger," explained Headmaster Lyonis.

"That I do know, and I also have the unique power to sense when people are lying, so do not test my questions…" suggested the torturer ominously. "What you said was true, sadly. Now, which of the students among these… one… two… three… seven! Which ones were with the dragon in battle? They shall be executed immediately! Who knows what kind of trouble a spirit like that could cause in the future," said Reginald. Headmaster Lyonis tried to recall what happened to Marcus and Robbert. Then he remembered that they were the two that were coincidentally thrown away.

'Well, none of these boys were with the dragon, that's the truth," answered the headmaster. The goblin looked at the boys... confused. "What in heavens do you mean? Every student was captured, were they not?" asked Reginald.

"Well, it was coincidence that the boys who were with the gold dragon were separated from this very group. No one went after them," replied Lyonis, enjoying watching the goblin scratching his notes in his file. Reginald slumped into his chair sorrowfully. "Curses... truth again!" retorted the torturer, bored, since there was no torture involved yet.

Suddenly, Lord Kragg himself entered the chamber. Reginald jumped up and bowed. "Milord, what brings you to this cursed room?" asked the goblin nicely. "Oh! I just personally wanted to hear the answers, doctor," replied Kragg as he snatched up the piece of paper with Reginald's notes. The torturer yelped. "Oh! This is very depressing," said Kragg, shoving the paper back into Reginald's face. The goblin whimpered, fearing that Kragg was about to fly into a rage. "How exactly did vampire Drador die?" he bellowed, knowing that Drador was alive, but hiding it in the question. He didn't want to give away too much information. "Well, your majesty, none of us experienced it exactly as it was, but the gold dragon and other two students did. But we know what happened," explained Headmaster Lyonis. "Well, spit it out, you fool!" yelled Kragg, impatiently. It was in his nature to be this demanding of his servants and prisoners. "Drador's troupe, the vampires, were turned to stone. One of those vampires had earlier taught the students how to use some sort of stone-turning spell. They all crumbled to pieces, never to be revived again," headmaster Lyonis answered. Kragg grunted. The six former students looked at each other, remembering that they had learnt some spells. They quickly taught to Pierce too, as he hadn't a clue of what they meant.

"Hey, maybe we can use that spell on those two," whispered Scabber. "Exactly what I thought," replied Tippy. All the boys nodded in agreement.

One thing the boys did not know was that spells were not conjurable in the Stronghold. "The vampire overlord was destroyed by the gold dragon. The dragon blasted the vampire with firepower," continued the headmaster. "And what was left of the vampire?" asked Kragg. "He was reduced to a pile of ash, O' great Kragg" replied Lyonis. A wide grin spread across Kragg's face.

"Say that again?" Kragg said. "What? A pile of ash?" repeated Lyonis. Kragg didn't say anything. Reginald was irritated because he was supposed to be asking the questions. He was also a bit confused about some of the questions. All the boys nodded to signal that it was time to use the spell. "Mandstone!" they yelled together, and closed their eyes expecting something to happen. But nothing occurred. Kragg burst into a laugh, "Ha! He, ho! Ha! Foolish children! Spells do not work here!" snorted Kragg. The torturer joined in too, so Kragg wouldn't be cross with him. Headmaster Lyonis was mouthing something to the boys, perhaps asking them why they did that of all the things.

The boys looked ashamed. "Well, that's that. So long! Now you will be escorted to the arena, where you will suffer a painful death among my beastly pets. Be grateful you get a chance, for I was deciding to burn you humans at the stake" announced Kragg grinning. "Please, we will do anything!" begged Lyonis.

"I have no use for you pests. I will stand by my decision, unless you want to make things quick" said Kragg, gesturing at the torture implements. Reginald suddenly got excited, but Kragg had already exited the torture chamber. "He never lets me do the killing…" muttered the goblin. Headmaster Lyonis's face dropped. The boys looked terrified out of their wits. Reginald snarled anyway as he left the chamber. After a few minutes of silence between the group, Tudar, the big goblin, entered the chamber to escort the prisoners to the arena of the stronghold.

—◆—

15

The Truth about Drador the Overlord

Kragg marched down a long corridor that led to the mess hall. He pushed open the doors to see all the vampire councilors seated there. "Ah! Perfect! Just the vampires I was looking for," beamed Kragg. "Lord Kragg, what brings you here? Are we getting better rooms?" asked Rackor, sounding hopeful. "Sadly not, but I have collected the news from our prisoners. It is wonderful and also depressing. Simply, good, and bad," replied Kragg. Rackor's smile returned.

"Please, tell us the bad news," suggested Rackor. "Hmm, we don't have the right children who helped the gold dragon do you know what…" said Kragg, hanging his head low.

"What do you mean? Oh no! It cannot be… I remember spotting two random students being swiped away by a behemoth, while the others got captured! Lord, those two must have been them!" cried Rackor woefully. "Yes, yes, it is a problem, but the good news is that your instincts about Drador were right," continued Kragg. "You see, the prisoners gave information that once they saw Drador blown up into flames, only a pile of ash was left behind. Surely, you do know what that means," explained Kragg, sheepishly. The vampires were astonished with this news.

"Y-yes! It means he m-must have used all his might to… travel at the speed of light across the world!" yelled Vade the vampire.

"Precisely. Speed Lighting. It could have killed him, but a vampire so powerful can survive with the tiniest bit of power left in him or her," said Kragg.

(Speed lighting is a fast way to travel through the world. You have to be extremely powerful to do it, and even if you are, you can only do it once.)

"So, Drador is still out there," guessed Wusim. "Of course!" cried Kragg. "He shall soon join the forces of evil, once he is healed." finished Kragg, before breaking into diabolical cackling. "Hehheheheheheh!" The vampires joined in as well, as this seemed to be the right occasion to join in.

The paintings of the ancient rulers of Karabor on the wall, looking over the mess hall…

16

The Mountain Troll

Marcus, Robbert and Fiddlin were getting off the ship on Karabor. Plonk! "Ah! How nice it feels to be back in a warm place," said Fiddlin. After him, Marcus and Robbert clambered out of the vessel, struggling with their equipment and enormous weapons. "Perfect, we're on the east side. Hardly any guards here," said Fiddlin, as he helped Robbert from falling. "So, Fiddlin, which way is the Stronghold?" asked Marcus, looking around and feeling slightly dizzy. Fiddlin pointed straight ahead at a huge mountain. "Once we 'ave climbed that, we'd be on the top of the hold itself. Ye'll see," explained Fiddlin. "Oh! And about your friends… they might already be in the fighting arena, getting ready for the battle of their lives, so we'd better hurry. Any spontaneous ideas?" said Fiddlin.

"Well, I've been thinking about this for quite some time, and I say we go as quick as we can. Then, we can sneak into the arena… Since you're a goblin, Fiddlin, you can be our cover. It'll all work out once we set the fellows free and let some of the wild beasts out. We can escape with them, and be on our way." explained Marcus hopefully. Fiddlin thought a bit. "Good, but we'd have to improvise the plan on the way. The Stronghold's defenses are quite solitary. We can't just walk in, even as a goblin…" he said.

"Yes, well, I'm sure there are some ways you can show us, Fiddlin," suggested Marcus. "Indeed, there are," answered Fiddlin, stiffly. "The real question is, how will we get out? The guards will be everywhere by then. We'll just have to go with what comes before us!" yelled Fiddlin, loudly. After the short discussion, the company went forth towards the mountains, which held the mighty stronghold behind them…

Every few steps, they looked around to make sure they were safe. Karabor was populated with quite the number of dangerous creatures these days. Once they reached the base of the mountain, they brought out their crowbars, as they hadn't any other tools to stick into the rocky terrain. "Are you sure this is safe, Fiddlin? It's an enormous mountain, and I'm not very keen on heights either," called out Robbert, nervously. "Ye'll be fine, Rodert!" replied Fiddlin. "It's Robbert by the way!" exclaimed Robbert defensively, at the mistake Fiddlin had made with his name. Marcus chuckled softly, so that Robbert wouldn't hear. With that, they started to climb the mountain, crowbars in hand… About an hour passed before they arrived at an ancient looking cave. "Finally! My bones felt like they were eating me!" cried Robbert rejoicing the fact that they could get some rest after that ever-lasting climb.

"Hmm, I have a feeling this cave isn't empty," said Fiddlin, as he looked around suspiciously. "Why is that?" asked Marcus putting down his crowbar on the rocky surface. Fiddlin pointed to a pile of flesh and bones. "That looks fresh," confirmed Fiddlin, a little worried. "Oh! How can you know that?" asked Robbert kicking an old pile of boulders. "Erm, why does this boulder feel like… hard skin?!" he wondered. Suddenly, the boulders started to move. Marcus got up from the floor and stood next to Fiddlin, sword in hand. "Oh no! Maybe it is." Fiddlin murmured. Now Robbert had fallen over as he took a step back. He lifted himself up and ran towards where Marcus and Fiddlin were. It was clearly visible that it was no pile of boulders, as the thing was now standing on two fat legs. The creature's head was turned to the other side, so it couldn't see them yet. Suddenly, terrible gas burst out from the monster's bottom. As it blew off, a terrible stench filled the cave. Fiddlin closed his eyes, while his nostrils flared. Marcus made a disgusting face and covered his nose. Robbert, however, coughed (a bit too loudly).

Immediately, the creature turned around and spotted them. Marcus turned to Robbert, who was still coughing like a horse. Fiddlin looked up at the snarling monster who had just passed very rude gas.

"Troll!" cried Fiddlin, as he drew his dagger. The troll charged at them. Fiddlin acted fast and shoved the boys and himself out of the way.

The troll's meaty arm smashed into the wall instead, narrowly missing Fiddlin's head. "We have to jump out of the cave!" called Fiddlin who got up with the boys and ran to the other side of the cave. "Are you kidding?!" the boys yelled in a unison. "Oh! Trust me if yeh want to live! It'll be okay!" replied Fiddlin as he made a leap for the entrance of the cave. He simply jumped out. The boys too shrugged and dived out of the cave. The troll drew back from the entrance, astonished. It had just missed its snack for the day… Plonk! Marcus and Robbert landed from their fall eventually. "H-how are we alive?" groaned Robbert.

"We're on sand! It's the sand that saved our lives, though my body is a bit sore," explained Marcus. "Told yeh it would work," crowed Fiddlin, rubbing his eyes which were full of sand. "How did you know we'd land on sand?"

"Well, you see, I'd been keepin' track of how we were moving. According to my memory, we were climbing the mountain diagonally, which led to a different part of the mountain. It had to be a change of terrain, so I guessed it would be a bit of desert in the area," said Fiddlin. "We're also closer to the Stronghold now. From here, if we go on with swift feet, an hour and a half, and we should be there," he explained.

The three of them sat down and ate remains of a bit of old bread, and then set out for the mighty Stronghold.

17

The Findings of Lobje, Tudar and Stoup

Creek! Lobje, Tudar and Stoup finished the council meeting in the grand hall and headed for the daily scout patrol. The three goblins worked together on ambushing tactics and strategies. Lobje took the lead, which meant he had the smartest brain. Tudar was the muscle, and Stoup was all speed and stealth. The three of them together made a very strong force of the stronghold. The goblin chieftains were very loyal to their king, and would give their lives for his majesty.

"Hope we get some prisoners back today, eh. Our reputation amongst the other goblins has been dropping at a terrible rate. It's unacceptable," Stoup said. Lobje agreed. Tudar opened the side door into the throne room. There were many goblins, all waiting for Kragg himself to arrive… The chieftains headed to the gates, where a guard inside pulled a rope hard, which worked the portcullis. The other guard unlocked the second gate before the portcullis, and the three goblins marched out, weapons in hand. They aimed to scout most of the land every day, and find wandering helpless goblins or enemies to send to lord Kragg. In recent times, they had not been very successful, and they did not think today would be any better…

After half an hour, the goblins were bored and tired. "Come on, yeh stupid rocks! Show us somethin' useful," yelled Stoup, annoyed. "Patience my feral friend. I am getting the feeling that something is around here. It be the chills, up the spine eh," replied Lobje suspiciously.

Shortly later, Tudar spotted a ship on the shore, which happened to be the one Marcus, Robbert and Fiddlin had come on a while ago. Lobje, Tudar and Stoup had come a short way around, only a few creatures important or ancient would know of. "Over there!" grunted Tudar, pointing at the rust-bucket. "Aha!" exclaimed Stoup. Lobje grinned. They hurried towards the vessel to inspect it for clues.

"Look for any outsiders or riches, however, this ship seems utterly abandoned," instructed Lobje, who jumped aboard the vessel. He walked straight for the captain's quarters. Stoup went down to the below-deck and Tudar rummaged through the barrels and piles of drums. Lobje sat down on a chair in the captain's quarters and looked at a familiar map. He saw the different lands and seas but stopped when he saw the travel indications. This was peculiar, as the black dots seemed to be starting from Necropolis Land Fall. "Strange, this was like our course from Necropolis to…" murmured Lobje. The indications ended in Karabor! "Well, good news, but what kind of fools would leave their map in the ship. Really strange," said Lobje to himself. He spotted a name on the edge of the map, which read, *THE PROPERTY OF FIDDLIN-GOBLIN.*

Lobje thought for a moment…

Fiddlin? Fiddlin! I know that name! Traitor! Coward!" yelled Lobje, recklessly. He got up from his chair. He believed that Fiddlin was mostly likely left behind in Necropolis and has now come back to the Stronghold for revenge on his brothers. "What a fool!" added Lobje, as he snatched the map and made his way to the door. He took one last look around, and suddenly spotted some hair on the floor. "Another clue, eh." He picked up the smidgen of hair, brought it close to his nose, and inhaled its smell…

He now knew exactly what kind of forces Fiddlin was forming. "Humans. Children!" cried Lobje, breaking into an evil grin. After a pause, map, and hair in hand, Lobje exited the room. Stoup and Tudar were seated on a bunch of barrels. "Ah! Lobje, erm we sadly did not uncover anything… but did you, eh?" asked Stoup clueless. "Oh! Yes. Do you remember that fellow Fiddlin?" asked Lobje. "You mean that small one, like me? Yeah," answered Stoup. "Yes, I think he was mistakenly left behind in Necropolis, not that it matters, but he has traveled back here to take revenge on us," said Lobje in a huff, handing the map to Stoup. Lobje showed them the hair. "He has some fellows helping him," added Lobje.

"H-humans? More of em?!" a confused Stoup asked. He could smell the hair from quite a distance with his sharp nose. "Absolute. Humans are on the run in Karabor," answered Lobje. Tudar stood up looking grim. "Therefore, we shall find them," boomed Tudar, in his deep, petrifying voice.

"We must take this matter into our own hands and not trouble Kragg with more thoughts. Nothing is stopping us from it. Let us head back, closer to the Stronghold, so we can catch them as they reach closer." instructed Lobje. And with that, the three of them set off, back to the mountains…

———•—•◦—•———

18

Let Battle Commence

Clang! Headmaster Lyonis, Tippy, Mar, Malop, Prith, Flipa, Scabber and Pierce had been thrown into a cell in the arena. It had a large steel gate, which a goblin locked, so there was no chance of anyone escaping. From tiny gaps, between the bars, the prisoners could see the arena, where others were torn apart. "I am truly sorry m' boys. Now we will die in this bloody forsaken arena," said Lyonis. "I'd never thought I'd die like this. I thought I'd die a hero, but more as a prisoner I shall," said Flipa. The other boys stared at Flipa, annoyed. Then, suddenly, a loud sound echoed in the arena, and caught everyone's attention. Bong! Bong! Bong! It came from the top, where the royalty sat. Kragg was sitting there bonging a large gong, which signaled it was time for the fight to begin. All the boys, including Headmaster Lyonis, jumped up and stuck their eyes through the gaps of the cell to get a view of the arena.

A large gate on the opposite side opened, like a portcullis, revealing a poor little goblin with a tiny axe. Malop felt sorry for him, as the creature was shivering with fear, even as he tried to get a good grip of the axe. Then, suddenly, there was a huge Screech, and another set of bars from the side opened. An enormous wyvern emerged…

"It's a wyvern! About seven or eight out of ten on the danger scale," pointed out Tippy, feeling all goody-two-shoes about his knowledge. "Oh no!" cried Malop staring at the beast's scaly skin. The wyvern arched its head up, looking at the puny goblin in front of it. The goblin didn't look very brave… it trembled forward, looking like a meatloaf that's about to be cut in half. The wyvern, meanwhile, started to shake its frills down its neck. Tippy knew what was happening, as usual, "Oh! Yes, the wyvern's deadliest weapon is…" explained Tippy, but couldn't finish his sentence because the wyvern had already demonstrated it.

The beast hurled a jet of fumes and poison at the goblin. Covered in the gooey mixture, the tiny goblin slowly started melting, like an ice cube in the summer. After a few moments of hissing, the only remains of the goblin were a puddle of sludge that looked like gunk and manure. "Hurrah!" yelled the crowd, applauding the wyvern. "I never thought I'd see it for real. Revolting," stated Tippy. The boys and the headmaster were shocked.

After the wyvern was chained up and transported back into its cell, and the acid cleared up, the boys and Lyonis slumped back into the ground. They heard screeches from the wyvern's cage, as it was whipped into calming down after it's deadly attack.

Then, Kragg spoke, "Boring! What a stupid battle! It hardly lasted a minute. Next time, we need some stronger prisoners, I say. What do yeh all think?" The crowd roared in agreement. "Good, good. Yeh hear that guards? Next time do not bring us some lousy villagers from goblin market that stole a coin or two. That goblin looked ill anyway. Well, whatever it was, the creature needed to be ended of its misery," continued Kragg. The crowd broke into maniacal cackling and laughter.

"Heh, now for our next battle, we have some newcomers we haven't seen in Karabor for a long, long time…" explained Kragg grinning away. Moments later, the guards marched over to the cell of Headmaster Lyonis and the students. "Oh no…" whispered Malop. "We have to fight now, don't we?" asked Pierce woefully. "Yes, boys. Whatever you do, try not to die," instructed the headmaster. Some of the students nodded uneasily, while the others looked like they were going to faint of fear. The guards quickly opened up the cell. "Oy humans! Your turn to die. Pick yeh weapons from this collection of battered ones," explained a guard, throwing a pile of old weapons on the ground. The boys picked up axes, swords, and maces. Lyonis, however, took a silver shield, as clear as glass. When he looked into it, he saw his old, bearded self. "Hmm, interesting," he thought. They slowly stepped into the arena… then, Kragg spoke, "I give you… the humans!" The seven students and Lyonis revealed themselves to the crowd. Most of the goblins were gasping and wondering, while some others were snorting and booing their heads off. "Boo!" "Humans?!" "Why?" "Ridiculous!" The boys made their way to the center of the arena, hanging their heads low, so they didn't see the disrespectful crowd.

"Now, now, that's enough. They shall be battling one of our most feared creatures here… Give a warm welcome to…" paused Kragg for suspense. In front of the prisoners, a cell opened. Out slithered a huge lady. Waist down, she had a snake's body and tail. Her hair blew furiously in all directions, quite impossibly.

Then, the others noticed it was not hair but snakes on her head. "Medusa!" yelled Kragg, finishing his sentence. The crowd roared. "Holy snakes! Whatever you do, do not look into Medusa's eyes.

One stare, and you'll turn to stone," said Prith. "Goodness, what else might we do?" cried the headmaster, backing away and lowering his head. The Medusa slowly started to slither towards the boys. "Well, just keep your head low and draw back. The Medusa has no other weapons, so we might be able to tire her," explained Scabber. The others followed and ran for the sides of the arena.

"Ready… set… fight!" bellowed Kragg, as he signaled for the battle to start. The Medusa made her way towards the humans. The boys looked rather stupid, jumping around with their heads hanging low. They hopped to the sides, escaping the slithery monster. "Hiss!"

"Boo!" "Fight! Fight! Fight!" yelled the crowd.

Kragg looked rather stumped. The boys continued to dodge the Medusa's blows. Then, the Medusa got fed up, turned around, and slithered the other way, hoping to catch the humans off guard, as they would run right into her hands…

She silenced her snake-filled head and waited for the boys to come closer. "Keep on going boys! Don't let her get you!" exclaimed the headmaster. Suddenly, the hissing re-commenced. Headmaster Lyonis lifted his head a teensy bit and saw the green hag in front of them! "How is she suddenly here?!" exclaimed Prith confused. The group started backing up, forming a line behind the headmaster. "Steady boys… steady…" said Lyonis retreating slowly. The Medusa was getting closer and closer. "Oh no! This is the end!" yelped Malop.

The crowd watched attentively, amazed at how long the humanoids had managed to survive, of course, they knew the group weren't going to last much longer. "Urgh!" grunted the headmaster, getting ready with his shield. The Medusa raised her hand, ready to strike him down, but Headmaster Lyonis was quick to lift his shield and stop her. The boys expected to hear a loud clang of collision, but there was no sound. "What?" wondered Tippy, slowly looking around to see what had happened. The headmaster lowered his shield, to see a statue in place of the Medusa! "How is this p-possible?" spluttered Flipa regaining his senses.

"Wait a minute, could you show me that shield sir," requested Scabber, walking up to Lyonis. The crowd was dumbfounded by this battle, as they all looked down in awe. Kragg was speechless. Scabber quickly checked the headmaster's shield. "Silver and as clear as glass! It must have gone like this. Once you held up your shield, the Medusa must have seen her own reflection and when she did so, she saw her own very eyes before her. She must have turned herself into stone without realizing it, because anything turns to stone from a medusa's glaze, including herself!" explained Scabber, knowledgeably. Normally this would be a statement from Tippy, who frankly didn't have a clue about it. "Headmaster, you are a hero!" added Prith. Scabber took the shield and catapulted it into the statue. The stone broke into a thousand pieces. "Now, we can be sure she's harmless," said Scabber.

Most of the crowd now started cheering for the boys and Headmaster Lyonis, except the grouchy ones of course…

No prisoners had ever survived the arena's monsters in a hundred and sixty-three years! Kragg was shocked but looked very hostile. The boys and Lyonis walked around the arena with pride, until the guards scurried in and forced them back to their old cell. As they walked out, the crowd continued to applaud the humanoids.

Kragg wasn't pleased one bit, so the cheering died down after a few moments. "Wow, that was incredible!" said Pierce. "Hurray for the headmaster!" added Pierce. Headmaster Lyonis smiled with joy. He hadn't felt one bit of happiness since they had arrived in Karabor.

When they were locked up in their cell, a guard whispered to them, "Just because yeh won one battle, doesn't mean it be the end. Ye got to battle till yeh die. The monsters will become more fearsome and stronger." Another guard said, "Yeah, yeh definitely won't survive another one. You've gotten the king of the Stronghold mad now, you did. Don't expect too much respect after this battle much longer." The boys took this seriously and started to look worried again. Their cell was locked, and the guards returned to their posts. Back in the arena, Kragg announced, "I am terribly sorry, my fellow subjects, the arena is closing for some time. Without further ado, I shall be leaving now." The crowd wasn't very pleased. "Aww! Why?! NO! Boo! We want blood!" yelled the goblins. Kragg didn't bother, and left for the stronghold.

19

Two Little Humans and a Goblin

"Huff! Huff! Huff!" Marcus, Robbert and Fiddlin waded through a thick forest. Leaves and vines covered everything around, making it a lot harder to see. Fiddlin had to use his knife and cut through the leaves to be able to even move. After about fifteen minutes, they came to a clearing. It was more rocky plains. "Aha! We must be murderously close to the Stronghold. I know these parts by me heart. Follow me," instructed Fiddlin, who put his finger in the air. Then, he licked it and made a sound of serenity, "Ahhh!" The boys realized he was tasting the wind, and seeing if they were in right direction. Fiddlin started moving his finger in all directions, and then started walking along. Marcus and Robbert followed closely. For a little while, they were sprinting as there seemed to be nothing around. Suddenly, a watchtower appeared in sight. "Get behind!" called Fiddlin quickly, pointing to a boulder a few steps away. Marcus, Robbert and Fiddlin crouched behind the boulder, and eyed the tower. Fiddlin explained, "There be always only one goblin on a watchtower, unless it be a guard-tower, which has five goblins, some wolves, and a troll. This tower, thankfully, be a watchtower with the one goblin, so maybe we can shoot the fellow from over here." Marcus readied an arrow steadily on his bow, but Fiddlin stopped him quickly.

"Wait! We can't just fire arrows anywhere! We need that fool to be in clear sight!" he yelled. Marcus lowered his bow and waited impatiently. Several minutes passed, then finally a fat goblin appeared in sight, scanning the perimeter.

He was at the top of the tower walking around. "Fire!" called Fiddlin, as Marcus hoisted his bow and let go of the string. The arrow went straight to the goblin's head, killing him instantly. "Whoa! Good shot, Marcus!" cried Robbert. The goblin started to tilt, about to plummet onto the floor.

Instead, the foolish thing bashed itself into the bell on the tower, and that made a loud sound. Gong! The bell broke off and clattered to the floor, the dead goblin with it. The two boys and Fiddlin were too scared to speak. "S-someone must have heard t-that!" cried Robbert worriedly. "Urgh! It's all my fault. I should have shot him more carefully," Marcus admitted angry at himself. Fiddlin patted Marcus on the back and walked over to the side next to the tower. There was nothing but land in sight. An enormous mountain appeared in view, however. It seemed like it was concealing the entire road to the other side, so there was no way they could get around it. "Pity really, which route do we proceed from now?" wondered Marcus.

Of course, Fiddlin knew what to do. "This is it! Mountain Malaheim!" cried Fiddlin with glee. "What's Mountain Malaheim?" asked Robbert curiously. "The mountain that divides that land from the Stronghold, of course! If we climb it, we'd be very close to the Stronghold. If we happen to reach the summit, which is quite high actually, we'll be scuttling on the roofs of the hold itself," explained Fiddlin, who was very eager now. "Wonderful! Then we probably won't be spotted!" said a relieved Robbert. "Well, we don't have any other options, so let's move swiftly, before someone who heard that bell comes along for a stroll." supposed Fiddlin. They began to make their way to the foothills of the mountain from where they could begin their climb. "Argh!" shrieked Marcus, as he struggled with holding on to the rocks. This mountain's terrain was too rocky, so it wasn't quite useful to use the crowbars, so they had to climb with no support. Marcus's foot was quite sore from all the running that they had endured.

"Help!" yelped Robbert as a sudden gust of dusty wind made him lose his balance and fall to the ground. Marcus stumbled down as well from tiredness. It was a few moments before Fiddlin realized that he was the only one climbing the mountain. "Boys? Would yeh hurry up and climb already! We do not want ta' squander our precious time resting about and feeling sorry for ourselves, do we? Get at it would yee?!" scolded Fiddlin, sternly. He waited a few seconds. No reply came back. He turned around and tried to spot the boys in the dusty air, but he couldn't see them, or anything for that matter. This was curious as the two of them were never this quiet. Fiddlin jumped down from the mountain to the ground, landing hard on his feet. "Boys?" he called, as he waged through the misty air, barely able to keep his eyelids open. Suddenly, he tripped over something that felt very strange indeed. It felt fleshy like a… leg…

"Arghhh!" yelled Fiddlin as he fell face-first on the ground.

Fiddlin tried to stand up but halted when he came face to face with an evil, murderous snarl. Out of nowhere, a large rock knocked him on the head, and he fell over more, this time unconscious. The last thing he heard was, "Tie em up Tudar! Use those big rope things around the mouths as well."

* * *

Marcus blinked his eyes open. The last thing he saw before being knocked out with a rock or something was a familiar-looking creature. "Ah! Finally! I was starting to think we hit em too hard with that rock," an unfamiliar voice said. Marcus came to his senses, to find himself tied up to a tree! He glanced around and wasn't very surprised to see Robbert and Fiddlin tied up on a couple of other trees. Moments later, he spotted a collection of very odd looking… goblins. Of course they were.

One was tall, strong, and as fat as a fat bear. The other was thin and short and looked like it could scale a tree within seconds. This was all very confusing for Marcus to take in so quickly, after that horrendous blow he got on his nut.

Marcus tried to speak, but only muffled-up words came out of the real question he has asked. Well, he realized the bindings across his mouth a bit too late, "Whurr err uuh?" Of course, what he meant to say was, "Who are you?"

Then, he noticed another goblin on the side who was tall but quite thin. He looked like the leader from Marcus's opinion, which is quite right. "Yeh have ropes on yer mouth, child. Nothin' ain't comin' out of those bonds," said the leader-looking goblin. Me name's Lobje. I have my partners, Tudar and Stoup. Yer goblin comrade might recognize us."

Confused, Marcus and Robbert stared at Fiddlin, who thought for a moment or two.

"Y-yes I do! My fellow chieftains!" blurted out Fiddlin astonished, but, of course, the others could only understand, "Rrrmph a drr! Murr frerorr chrffftnns!"

Lobje sighed and sent Stoup to untie the ropes on Fiddlin's mouth so they could understand what he was saying. Stoup did as he was told and brought out a knife.

For a moment, Stoup looked like he might kill Fiddlin, but Stoup simply hacked the ropes open for Fiddlin to speak. "Woah! Thank yee," called out Fiddlin, trying to catch his breath again. "Yes. I remember you my friends. Yer the high goblin chieftains who fought alongside the army of the Stronghold during various battles…"

Part 3

Escape from Karabor

20

More Prisoners for Kragg

"Well, I'm glad you remember us, you traitor!" accused Lobje, folding his arms. Fiddlin was furious now, "Traitor? What do yeh mean? I've just come 'ere to return to the Stronghold and help these humans who travelled with me. I just need to help them rescue some friends of theirs, and they'll be off, for the devil's sake!" explained Fiddlin. Lobje looked even more astonished now. "Yeh wouldn't dare it! Breaking out some prisoners of Kragg's? Yeh mucky thug! That makes thee a bigger traitor than ever, you rogue!" Fiddlin couldn't wriggle out of this now, but he could argue. "Well, it be your own fault that the army left me behind. Could yeh not have cared to remember that I was left behind?"

These two very children here were smart enough to strike a deal with me and 'elped me get back 'ere. I did what had to be done, or else I would be found and skinned alive by those people in that stupid village we took down!"

Lobje couldn't listen anymore, "Enough! You've always been such a fool, Fiddlin. Always running away from the big battles. Getting a chance to be one of us chieftains, and throwing it away like a pebble… Come on, Tudar! Take them off the barks and carry 'em back to the hold." Marcus and Robbert tossed around nervously. Tudar strode over to them and yanked them off the trees, ripping apart some of the bonds with his elephant sized hands. Then he tended to Fiddlin and did the same, stripping him off and putting him on his shoulder with the other two.

Fiddlin didn't make a peep, as he was still angered with his fellow goblins. Stoup led the way back to the Stronghold, while Lobje and Tudar followed closely behind. Climbing up the huge mountain needed quite the effort, but the goblins thought of a quick way up. They tied some extra ropes attached with hooks and launched them up on the mountain and climbed it with ease. "Behold, we be inventing the hook that grapples you up a mountain without killing you! What should we be naming it?" Lobje wondered, with their new invention in his grasp. "Erm, Grappling hook?" suggested Robbert. "Yes! I was just about to say that…" retorted Lobje, giving Robbert a nasty look. Even Tudar, who was carrying the three prisoners, was able to progress. Shortly, they were standing on the mound just above the Stronghold's ancient turrets of old…

Kragg entered the throne room and greeted all the goblins waiting for his arrival. He neatened up and headed for the arena as it was battle time. He had planned a nasty line up. The idiot humans were in for a horrifying shock!

21

The Second Round

Screech! "Yeahhhhhh!!!" The goblin crowd roared as a huge bird called a roc was slowly being ripped alive by a wild troll, feather by feather.

Slump! The bird dropped to the ground, dead. The crowd hooted as the troll lifted the dead roc above his head. Kragg clapped along, praising his own kin. "Magnificent, what a performance by this troll! I see the guards finally stepped it up. Creature versus creature. Outstanding," said Kragg, even though it was his own idea. He didn't like the idea of his guards being killed by angry goblins in the stands… The guards took a bow, stealing the glory, even though no one really cared. The guards rushed out into the arena, whips in hand. The ogre wasn't very happy to go back already. The beast slowly trudged towards its cell, while the guards whipped its back hard. The crowd cackled away at this cruel sight. Back in the human's cell, the boys and the headmaster were shivering with fear…

"What gruesome creatures. Poor bird," said Malop sorrowfully.

"Oh! Don't be very sorry for that bird. It's kind have killed countless numbers of livestock in most villages… it's a good thing they captured it," said Tippy. "Everyone, remember what those guards said, we're in for the fight of lives, so we have to get prepared," announced Pierce. "He's right, let's look around the cell. Maybe there's some bits we could use," agreed Mar. So, they searched through the rocks and stones, searching for something worthwhile. Minutes later, they found a black chest peeping out of the ground. "What in the world?" cried Malop. "Treasure! It's ours for the taking!" Everyone was astonished. How could they not have seen it before! There was a little message carved on top of it that read, WHICHEVER SOUL OF GOODNESS FINDS THIS CHEST, INSIDE THEY MAY FIND THE SPARE KEY! USE IT WELL!

There was silence for a few moments. "Strange. Who would put a key in here that the goblins could find so easily?" wondered Scabber.

"A wizard who was trapped earlier in this cell, most likely. A spell must make it only visible to the greater good's eyes," answered Tippy. Prith and Flipa tried to heave out the chest. "Huh? That was pretty easy," said Scabber. To make things simpler, the chest didn't need to be unlocked. The boys opened it straight away.

The key was as good as new. "Well… this is amazing luck that has been brought upon us! But where does this 'spare key' lead to?" questioned Pierce. Headmaster Lyonis picked it up and walked to the cell door. He inserted the key into the slit, and it fit perfectly. But the headmaster didn't open the doorway, because there was another battle about to begin, and they didn't want to get caught. The boys were celebrating now. "Yes! We can escape," cried Mar. Fortunately their happiness lasted about two minutes. Suddenly, Kragg's voice echoed, "I inform everyone here today that the fight coming up will go down in history, as the puniest forces take on the greatest of them all!" The crowd fell silent. Was it to be? Was everyone's worst nightmare coming true? Two guards with a bundle of weapons walked into the human cell. "Told you so," they said to the boys and the headmaster. Headmaster Lyonis threw the key to the side so the goblins wouldn't see it and hid the chest under some rocks. As usual, the boys had to pick their own weapons, and they seemed to be more improved this time. The sky started darkening strangely. Loud screeches could be heard from the other end of the forsaken arena.

The boys chose their weapons carefully. Some took the big battle-axes, and others the bows and arrows. A couple of them took longswords as well. If it was a big fight, you're going to need big weapons… Again, Lyonis took the strangest of things left. A leather piece of padding and a whip along with a huge black stick. "Are yeh sure, old man?" asked the guards confused. "Oh! Let me choose, you stupid old bats," Lyonis snapped. The guards snorted and scurried away with the weapons. The cell door opened behind them, and out stepped the eight human warriors. "Here comes… the humans!" bellowed Kragg, restraining himself to not call them ugly. The crowd roared for them as they had survived their first round. "Will these newcomers succeed once more, or battle to their death?" questioned Kragg. Of course, the crowd chanted, "Death! Death! Death! Death!" The boys and the headmaster seemed terribly afraid now, but abruptly, lightning struck the arena, terrifying the crowd into silence.

In the columns where the goblins were seated was a mysterious figure in a hood and cloak walking down the long stairwell. Who was he? Was he a goblin or not?

There was a loud boom, as the crowd settled back into their seats. Thump! Thump! A portcullis opened in front of the humans. "Everyone, keep calm," said Headmaster Lyonis trying to not stress the children. The creature that stood behind the portcullis wasn't very patient. It was as hungry as a wolf hunting. The blood-longing creature grabbed the portcullis and broke it in two. SCREEAACCHHH! The creature stepped out of the darkness revealing itself. The crowd gasped in horror. Kragg laughed softly. The humans were struck by terror. A white, rough skinned, battered and bruised mythological creature reared up. Huge red eyes it had, and fangs that could pierce iron. The black scales along its back and tail were easily the scariest of any monster. It was the Nightmare Dragon of Dracula, the ancient king of necromancy! The first thing it laid it's eyes on, were the humans…

22

Help has Arrived

Slam! The portcullis shut as Lobje, Tudar and Stoup walked in with the new prisoners. Goblins sitting around in the throne room were astonished. "More humans? How can this be possible? Is it human-hunting season?" one of them asked. They were all very confused. "Not to worry, there be a goblin prisoner as well. One of our own soldiers who betrayed us and was caught helping these pests to break out their friends from our clutches," announced Lobje.

The crowd of goblins gasped. "What a coward!" they shouted. "Yes, agreed. Now, where is Lord Kragg?" demanded Lobje. "Oh, he is currently in the arena, chieftain. Big fight going on there. One of them big beasts," said a goblin. "Ah! Wonderful, you humans can see yer friends die," said Stoup. "No!" cried Marcus and Robbert.

They didn't say more, as there were too many goblins around. They had to admit though, the Stronghold was quite the structure…

"Since Kragg is not around, we be taking these humans to their cell. The goblin may as well go in with them, as there ain't much space left in the arena columns. It's been a packed day," two guards spoke among themselves. Lobje, Tudar and Stoup left the prisoners to the guards, and looked to their own work, proud of all that they had accomplished.

The guards lifted Marcus, Robbert and Fiddlin by their legs and took them to the arena. After a short walk, they arrived behind all the action at the columns and pushed the prisoners into the cell. "Stop!" cried Fiddlin. "Keep quiet you, or I'll pull off your arms," said one guard. The guards locked the door and left. "Well, this is just great. Now what?" asked Robbert. "Hey, look!" Marcus pointed at the arena. He could see Prith, Scabber, Flipa, Mar, Malop, Tippy and Pierce along with the headmaster! "Hooray! It's them! We found them!" he shouted with joy.

"Don't be too happy. Look. They be battling. Oh devils… 'tis the nightmare dragon! There's no killing it!" said Fiddlin worriedly.

"Oh no! What do we do? It looks a lot like what you describe, Fiddlin," the boys said, their hearts pounding violently. "Hold up, what's that?" Marcus pointed to a little key on the floor. "Erm, I wonder what that leads to? Hopefully useful," said Robbert. "Oh! Maybe your friends might have left it behind for us," Fiddlin said as he grabbed the key and shoved it into the door leading into the arena. It fit! "Okay, so now we know we can get out and fight for your friends," said Fiddlin. "Yeah! Good job Fiddlin! Let's go quick," Marcus said. "Wait, we don't have weapons. Are you two sure yeh be riskin' yer lives for yeh friends?" Fiddlin asked. Marcus and Robbert looked at each other. They could see that their friends were trying to shoot down the dragon with their bows, but the dragon was just waiting, like it was firing up or something. "Of course, we're sure. Open it up…" the boys said with a smile. Fiddlin did as he was told and pulled the door open. They stepped out and shut the door behind. The guards noticed them immediately and tried to get to them, but the three of them ran like the wind and jumped into the arena. The guards didn't dare to catch them now, as the dragon was too scary to get near to. The crowd looked on in awe. How were there more humans? And even a goblin!

What was it doing with humans?! Kragg's eyes widened menacingly. What on earth was going on? No one had told them that there were more prisoners arriving. The crowd thought it was a part of the battle and kept cheering on.

Fiddlin regretted why he had agreed to this, but now that he was here, what could be better than fighting the nightmare dragon itself. "Marcus, Robbert! You both are alive?" The boys called while trying to focus on the dragon. "Yes! We journeyed here to save you all. But it seems a bit late now. We're very sorry," Marcus and Robbert said. "It's alright. At least we'll fight alongside one last time," said Headmaster Lyonis. Marcus and Robbert readied their fists for battle. "Err, what about me?" said Fiddlin. "Oh! Yes! Everyone, meet Fiddlin. He's a goblin from the Stronghold who helped us get here. Long story," said Marcus, introducing Fiddlin. "Hello! Nice to meet you Fiddlin. Good luck," some of the boys said as they fired arrows at the dragon. The strange thing was that the dragon just stood there with its wings folded.

It's neck, however, seemed to be giving off odd sparks, and there was some blue and purple power running through its veins. "I think it's readying up, or something," guessed Mar. "Whatever it is, it doesn't look good for us."

"Oh! Yes! The dragon will first attack with them fumes of blue and purple beam of utter darkness. It extracts its enemies' souls, making it more commanding over the enemy. As soon as it puffs, just try and dodge, is all me thoughts can say," said Fiddlin.

The company did as they were told and as soon as the dragon let out the blinding fumes, they rolled to the sides, hiding behind rocks. The dragon kept directing its power at them, without a second's break. "Yes, another thing is it won't stop the exhaustion until it has captured at least a mere two or three souls," explained Fiddlin. "You tell us now? What would you have us to do then?!" called the headmaster. Fiddlin replied, "Haven't a clue…"

After a while, the dragon got tired of its efforts and rested for a moment. It then turned to the guards on the side and blasted a fence. The goblin guards started trembling. The dragon succeeded in finding them in its grasp, making them drop their weapons and levitate in the air. Their eyes turned completely white as the beam sucked their evil souls out of their bodies. When the collection was complete, a white orb flew out of the goblins' mouths and into the dragon's noses. Boom! Immediately, the dragon flashed more colors, feasting its deadly eyes on the humans. "Not good, the dragon has its souls now! What a smart creature," said Marcus marveling at the nightmare. It didn't last too long, as the beast blew an inferno of blue flames, making a ring of it around the whole field. The humans wouldn't be able to run forever, as the fire started closing in on them.

"Now what?!" asked Malop yelping. Fiddlin told the boys who had bows to smoke their arrows in the fire and aim them at the dragon. It was time to give this beast a taste of its own fire. The boys did as they were told and set their arrows aflame. They hoisted their bows and fired at the dragon, aiming for its enormous head. The dragon screeched as some of them went into its eyes. The creature may have been temporarily blinded, but it still had an excellent sense of smell of blood. It came to its senses and started to create the infernos again. The boys took cover with the headmaster and Fiddlin behind some rocks, but they knew they couldn't keep this up much longer…

In the meantime, there was some action in the crowd as well. It was the mysterious figure from earlier creating a scene. Whoever it was, it started pushing goblins out of its way and rushed towards the wall separating the spectators from the arena. It jumped over the stone bricks, and landed on top of the glass roofs.

In no time, it was right above the battle standing with a magnificent sword, made of iron and bronze. The guards rushed from their posts and tried to stop the figure. But it was too late.

The figure was standing right on top of the glass where the dragon was and smashed a sword right into the unbreakable glass. What kind of sword was this? Within seconds, the glass cracked, and a perfect hole was created for the figure. Looking at the guards who were standing in awe, it said, "Goodbye…" It was a voice that didn't belong to a goblin. He dropped through the hole with ease.

He fell right onto the nightmare's back! The dragon took no notice, but the prisoners did. "Who in the world is that?! Is he mad?" cried Robbert. The others too looked quite shocked. The dragon continued snorting its blaze, as the figure got into position with his sword. The group couldn't see very well, but the figure's hood had fallen off. He had long black hair that rippled in the wind. It was a very familiar looking person…

He finally regained his balance, gripped his sword, and scraped it along the dragon's hide. The dragon let out a loud yelp as the warrior continued scratching skin off its back. Not long after, the human figure reached the end of the tail and almost cut it off, but not quite. The dragon fainted temporarily. The man got off the dazed serpent slowly. The crowd erupted in applause, thinking that it was all over. But that was folly for no one could kill the dragon so easily and even the man who tried to knew it. Kragg was dizzy at the sight of so many humans. "Stop all your whooping and joy, the dragon is merely knocked out. Give it five minutes, and there'll be a lot of dead humans on the field. The dragon stirred as the moments went by. The man jogged up to the prisoners. He bowed at them. The boys and the headmaster were blown away by his appearance. "Holy heavens!" they cried together…

———•●•———

23

How to Tame a Nightmare

"Sir Vlad?!" the boys and headmaster shouted together. "Yes, 'tis me, Vlad," said the swordsman. "But the last time I saw you, you were in hospital! How did you recover so quickly?" asked Marcus. "Well, you see, I creeped out. Late in the cover of night, I pulled off all my casts and I felt much better anyway, so I leaped out the window and headed straight for the docks. Borrowed a boat from an old friend…" explained Vlad. "Well, then, welcome back, Sir Vlad," greeted Headmaster Lyonis with a smile.

"So, did you kill the dragon?" asked Malop. "Well, no. I just temporarily dazed it. It should be back any moment. Hmmm, if only we had a stick…" said Vlad. "I do! I have a stick. Does it help in any way though?" interrupted the headmaster. Suddenly, Fiddlin joined in. "Oh, heavens you great old hag, why didn't you tell me earlier! What kind of coincidence is it that you have a large black stick?! Where did you get it?" cried Fiddlin. "Oh, the guards were handing out weapons and this was one of them. I didn't think it would be useful, but there weren't any swords left," replied the headmaster who was quite clueless.

No one really spoke for a moment. Then, Vlad said, "Well headmaster, black sticks can be converted into necropolision staffs! The Dracula himself used it to tame the nightmare." Mar cried: "Once again, headmaster, you're the hero!" The others agreed. What they all didn't notice was that there were guards coming in to get them, as the dragon was still down.

"Oh! Now, hold up, why is there a goblin here in the first place?" Vlad asked, drawing his sword. "No, Sir Vlad! He helped us. He's on our side," explained Marcus. Vlad put his sword back.

"Alright then. You, Goblin, take the headmaster and Robbert and teach Mr. Lyonis to use the stick. The rest of us will take care of these rotten creatures," said Vlad. Everyone nodded in agreement. The fire had died down a little bit, so Fiddlin led the headmaster and Robbert into a corner behind some rocks while the rest of the boys and Vlad went after the guards. But it wasn't only the guards they would be fighting. Kragg had ordered them to get the troll in as well. Meanwhile, in the crowds, the goblins were booing and cursing the humans. They were also shouting, "Get up, you useless slug! Fight! Foolish beast!" Behind the rocks, Fiddlin was teaching the use of the black stick to Lyonis. "So, all yeh have to do is first make the stick a staff. Now, this be a very ancient vampire spell. Don't ask me how I'd learnt it, or I might bite you. Go forth and yell… CLONEY SKULLION STAFF!" The headmaster repeated: Cloney skullion staff!" "You need to say it much louder, you fool! Like THIS!" shouted Fiddlin.

"Oh, alright, alright… CLONEY SKULLION STAFF!" recited the headmaster. Then, the stick made a weird sound and Boom! It had transformed into a skullion staff of the Dracula himself. "Good job! Now this not be the actual staff. But it has some traits. Very rare, these extreme black sticks. Only found in hell fall," explained Fiddlin. Headmaster Lyonis was proud of himself. There was a glowing red eye at the end of staff. It looked like it was the Dracula's forsaken blood eye. "Well, how do we get the dragon to wake up, by the way?" questioned Robbert, who was quiet all this while. "We have to shove the dark staff in its bloody eye. The glow is bright enough to get a sleeping renocentamin. Then, we have to make the eye on the staff stare into the dragon's own eye. That's how we be getting control of it," said Fiddlin.

Headmaster Lyonis remembered that he had some leather and a whip. "Wait, maybe we could make a saddle out of these," he said. Fiddlin stared for a few seconds, wondering how the old man always had the right tools. "Yes, great idea, Mr. Old man. But will it be big enough, be the question?" questioned Fiddlin doubting the idea. "No it won't, but I just need comfortable seating, that's all," said the headmaster, making things easier for the execution of the horrible task.

"If you say so old man," replied Fiddlin.

Meanwhile, the other boys and Vlad were losing the fight. The guards were really bulky and had tough armor and huge flails and spears. They flung their flails, which made it really hard for the boys to get away in time before the spikes hit.

One hit from those and you could say goodbye. The troll was also trying to smash the humans, using its large fists. "Urgh, what do we do Vlad?! We can't get at them properly from close and there isn't enough time to even get our bows ready for a ranged attack!" cried Marcus, who earlier borrowed a bow from Prith. Vlad kept fighting on. Then he thought of something. "Everybody, we actually don't really need to fight them, we just need to get out of the way in time. They'll probably get tired with those heavy weapons and by then the headmaster should be prepared to use the dragon on the guards. So, we really don't need to attack," said Vlad. The boys understood the plan and continued evading the guards carefully.

Kragg was observing all that was going on. He had noticed the black stick, as everyone else had too. "If only the stupid guards didn't hand over that black stick," he thought to himself. He didn't want the humans to get control of the dragon and then use him to destroy the whole stronghold, but things were looking out of hand now, so he sent his guards to round up the army for battle once more.

Headmaster Lyonis got really close to the dragon's eye. He started bonking the staff on its eye. "C'mon yeh thin son of a lizard! Git' to it!" cried Fiddlin. It did no good. On the other side of the arena, Tippy got in a good spot and no one was attacking him, so he got his bow out and tipped an arrow in the last remaining fires. He aimed it at the troll's head. Coincidentally, the monster bent down right at that time to reach for one of the boys who had stumbled to the floor. "Yaaaarrrgghh!!!" the beast screamed in pain as a fiery arrow pierced its rear end.

All the boys started sniggering as the monster pranced around, screeching while holding the little ragged cloth covering its behind.

"Ha! Ha! Ha!" Even Vlad's lips began to quiver. The laughing died down when the ogre turned around grimacing, and eyeing Tippy. "Run!" yelled Vlad. Tippy started retreating slowly, but the troll stomped towards him, revealing its yellow, blood-curdling crooked teeth. "Grarr!"

"Bang!!!" Headmaster Lyonis whacked the dragon's head again. The sound of the troll roaring in pain woke the nightmare immediately! Headmaster Lyonis, Fiddlin and Robbert were standing in front of it, it's eyes very wide open now. "Back away, back away! Slow and steady," said Fiddlin calmly.

The crowd roared as the dragon got up and spread its wings like a hawk. "Rrrrrrrrrrr…"

The dragon fixed its eyes on the three of them, and snarled. "Wait for me call, Lyonis, wait for it…" called Fiddlin. The blood nightmare dragon took a step towards them. "… and… now!" called Fiddlin. Lyonis drew the staff in the air and turned the red eye right towards the dragon's blood eye. The dragon started at the light. For some reason, the headmaster's hand started swaying from side to side. The dragon's eyes moved along with the staff. "Hypnosis!" thought Robbert, as he had read about it in an old book back at Dormando Towers. After a few minutes of this, the crowd fell silent, not understanding how this battle was so exciting. Then, the headmaster's mouth opened and out came his bright soul in a sphere. The sphere immediately broke into two and one half went back into his body the other half went into the dragon's mouth. Next, the dragon's mouth opened and out came its dark soul, broken in two, half of which went into Lyonis, and the other half went back into the beast. Now each of them had one combined soul. Then, all of a sudden, Bang! The dragon's eyes turned blue, and also the headmaster's himself.

"Oh god!" the headmaster huffed. The dragon let out a whimper. "Well done, old man! Yee now be a part of the dragon and the dragon be a part of yee. It's in your command now. I think we all know what we have to do." suggested Fiddlin. "Let's saddle it up, shall we?" started the headmaster, glancing at the battle going on. He used his hand to put the dragon in a lying position so they could easily attach the saddle and tie it up properly. Headmaster Lyonis was no longer just a headmaster. He was a dragon rider as well.

———•●•———

24

The Fall of the Arena

Chomp! Lyonis got the dragon to eat all the guards and knock out the troll as well. "Hurrah!" roared the crowd. Had they known that the humans were not going to go back into their cell, they would not have made a sound, but they would have screamed… Kragg was so afraid, he sounded the alarm. DONG! DONG! The goblins in the crowd were surprised and didn't know what would befall their forsaken arena…

"Hurrah for the headmaster!" cried Vlad and the boys. "Yes! Now let us be getting out of here!" cried Fiddlin. Everyone hopped on to the nightmare's bony back, while the headmaster started to converse with the dragon to get them out of the arena. But it was too late…

Goblin soldiers rushed in from all the columns, spears, axes, and swords in hand. They were followed by a number of trolls and ogres. Wolves surrounded the area, snarling at the humans. Kragg grinned, but he was still worried for his life. He vanished from the arena, hoping to find a safe place to hide in the Stronghold. A behemoth was loaded in, and the humans, the dragon and Fiddlin were suddenly surrounded! "Not good! What do we do, Vlad?" asked Robbert. Vlad told Headmaster Lyonis to surround them with fire. Lyonis commanded the dragon, who did as it was told. The army of the Stronghold slowly drew back, to escape the flames. Some goblins were unlucky, though, and were caught by the raging blaze.

Suddenly, one of them cried the battle cry and not caring for the flames before them, the army rushed in to chop the dragon's head down. The boys with bows were under Fiddlin's command to fire at them. Lyonis ordered the dragon to attack, and all the boys Vlad and Fiddlin then leaped off the dragon's back, weapons in hand. "YEAHHHH!!!" yelled the boys, as they plummeted to the battle of their lives.

They landed on the heads of their foes and fought bravely against the goblins. While the army was distracted with the group down below, the trolls, ogres and the behemoth charged towards the dragon and pinned it down to the floor. Headmaster Lyonis charged up the dragon quickly with the staff and the dragon blasted its way through. Headmaster Lyonis took the dragon up above and started causing havoc by breaking the glass and destroying the arena, making it rumble like an earthquake. Goblins in the stands ran for the exits, to escape the battle, while some took their chances, and jumped into the field for battle. The arena was crumbling, and the dragon was too strong for the trolls and ogres that tried to bring it down. "Good job, nightmare," whispered Lyonis. The dragon nodded in agreement. Then, the beast swooped down and fought the trolls and ogres to the death.

Vlad and the boys took on all the goblins while Fiddlin went one-on-one with the behemoth. Fiddlin scaled the behemoth as quick as he could and dug his blade into the side of the monster's head. He had tried this before, so he was not vulnerable to the big beast. The behemoth roared in agony, but it was not finished. It picked Fiddlin up from its back and brought him to the front of its large, ape-like face. At that moment, the behemoth inhaled deeply as some bug got stuck in his nose. Fiddlin got popped into the behemoth's nose! Dangling out, Fiddlin said to himself, "No one must ever know of this…"

* * *

The boys had managed to scare the goblins enough. "Draw back! Spare yeh lives, yeh fat cows!" yelled a goblin from the side. The army ran back, warning the Stronghold to build a full defense system. Lyonis landed the dragon near the group below. Fiddlin was panting on the side, covered in snot, as the behemoth puffed him out of its nose and scampered away to defend the hold. "What happened to you?" asked Marcus. "Nothing, nothing at all…" replied Fiddlin, cleaning himself up. "Yeah! We did it!" some of the boys called. "Don't get too excited," said Vlad. "We still need to get out of here," he continued. "I'm afraid that our friend Fiddlin will have to make the decision… Sir Fiddlin, would you allow we who stand before you to destroy the Stronghold?" asked Vlad.

Everyone's eyes turned to Fiddlin. Fiddlin didn't know what to do, but he did have one thought. "No, we should not have to be destroying the Stronghold. All we have to do is change the minds of them subjects. It is Kragg who makes us think that the good souls are wretched… and that be not true, I have learnt. We need 'ta make Kragg pack up and leave and crown a new leader of good mind," explained Fiddlin.

The humans understood. "And that ruler would be you?" guessed Lyonis. Fiddlin did not agree. The boys and Vlad agreed. "ME?! Not a chance…" cried Fiddlin, amused. "It has to be. You're the only goblin who is on the good side," said Marcus. "Yeah!" exclaimed the other boys. Fiddlin felt honored, but foolish. "I be having a better plan instead…" he said softly. "Your decision, Fiddlin. No time to waste, get on the back of the dragon already!" shouted Vlad climbing aboard with the headmaster.

"This is going to be quite the task." thought Fiddlin, as the dragon took off, soaring into the sky and crashing the glass. "Oi!" cried Fiddlin, as Lyonis laughed to himself. Lyonis directed the dragon to the main part of the Stronghold.

Part 4

Peace is Made

25

A New Era for Karabor

All the spectators rushed into Stronghold's throne room. Goblins of the army entered to room to calm things down, while Kragg got up on a small overlook above the throne. "My fellow goblins! The humans and the traitor are circling this very part of the Stronghold with that monstrous serpentine! Be calm! The army has sent the archers to guard the area!"

BASH!!!

The dragon flew into the room breaking it into two. The goblins yelped and rushed to get to the other side. "These archers?" Lyonis asked holding the archers by the scuff of their necks. The crowd of goblins gasped in horror. The humans and Fiddlin got off. Lyonis ordered the dragon to snarl at the goblins fiercely.

Suddenly, the army surrounded the humans from the back and sides. Kragg grinned. "One wrong move humans, and I warn you, the army will attack," he said.

"Wait!" shouted Fiddlin. "We come in peace! We will not hurt your people, unless you do to ours," explained Marcus. Fiddlin jumped onto the dragon's back, which stopped growling. This was a strange move from Fiddlin…

"All these years, have yeh all ever want a little' bit o' peace? Always, we be having to do all these things unnecessarily, like 'Go kill that fool!' or, 'Go take over that land over there!' Do we really be needing do everything told to us? Why can't we be livin' in peace and doing what we be pleasing and not kill everyone for the order? Because of them royals. All they do is make us do things that never really had to be done. We never had to destroy these them human villages. We were always just on the wrong side of the world," explained Fiddlin. All the goblins were confused, but also intrigued. Kragg was worried, and wanted to tell the army to attack, but it was pointless now.

"Them rulers think they have so much power and they make them subjects do all their dirty work. Rulers and subjects should not be different, for the devil's sake, in Karabor, there not should not even be royals, the way we have been havin' em for centuries. We be not deserving it, because all them royals have made us look like monsters and they humans call us... Dirty Pigs!" The crowd gasped. Never had they heard of humans that curse them. "Stupid, stupid royals! Places like Frohaven needs it, as they be having royals who make their land proper and not a land of treachery," continued Fiddlin, tired now of his explanations.

All the goblins were shocked. The army started putting their weapons down. Kragg was getting his subjects' attention now. "Ha! What a stupid little wart! Who would listen to that folly?!" cried Kragg. "We would..." said the goblins together, and turned back to Fiddlin. Kragg shut up after that. "So, what do yeh say, fellow goblins? We can start a new generation for the stronghold, or yeh all can continue to be the cowards yeh always have been," asked Fiddlin. The goblins were very eager at Fiddlin's thoughts.

All their lives they thought that the humans and the good creatures were terrible, and they wanted to rule everything and needed to be killed. For generations the royals had perpetrated these lies. Even the goblins most loyal to Kragg were bewildered with this turning news. Suddenly, Lobje, one of the chieftains of the Stronghold, cried, "How do we be knowing you are not lying?" Kragg was trembling now, and he knew he would not be able to hold this up much longer. "H-he is r-right. The r-royals are t-terrible here," said Lyonis, anxiously. "They control you! Look into your minds!" cried Vlad. The army, the subjects and the chieftains were convinced now. Suddenly, a goblin cried, "Kragg no more! Kragg no more!" Lots of goblins joined in, then the whole army, including the chieftains, joined in, "Kragg no more!!! Kragg no more!!! KRAGG NO MORE!!! **KRAGG NO MORE!!!**" Everyone in the room seemed to be chanting the same words. "I thought you'd become the ruler Fiddlin, but it seems like this is for the best…" said Robbert, smiling at his goblin friend. "Yeah!" cried the boys.

The goblins kept chanting, while some ogre and trolls outside discussed with each other. The biggest surprise was when the chieftains surrounded Kragg. "Sorry milord, or should I say, filthy goose butt!" yelled Lobje grinning. All the chieftains started kicking him one by one. "Birdy!" joined in Tootha. "Plump piggy!" screamed Dagger. Ivy and Crooked together said, "Blasted sack of cow fat!" while Peregrines shouted, "Son of the fattest snail!" "Empty-headed old tadpole!" screamed Rave. Stoup chimed in too: "Stupid baked pie!" while Tudar boomed, "Great farty elephant!" And it continued, as the crowd laughed as the humans rejoiced…

So, what happened to Kragg? The goblins locked him in the most secure prison cell of all in the bronze gate prison of Karabor (inaugurated by Kragg himself, a few years ago). And thus, the humans and Fiddlin became the heroes who were remembered in a new era of peace in Karabor. Fiddlin was named the high chieftain, to make some rules for the land along with his fellow chieftains.

Now the Stronghold's army led on good goblins who could summon the humans for help if they were ever under attack as the humans could too.

— •●• —

26

The Heroes Depart

After a series of many adventures in Karabor, it was time for the humans to depart. The boys, Lyonis and Vlad packed their weapons and headed to the borders of Karabor. "Hmmm, what an adventure we've had in Karabor. I wonder what's next," said Marcus. Lyonis saddled the dragon.

Suddenly, out of all the corners, goblins rushed towards them. They surrounded the humans. "What's happening?" asked Tippy. Then, Fiddlin came out, armed with all his gear. "I am departing from Karabor for now, my friends. I have set some rules and left the kingdom in the hands of the other chieftains. I will continue with all of you in your many battles to come…" announced Fiddlin to the humans. "That is wonderful!" called the boys. Fiddlin was a formidable and skilled fighter, and a very wise guide as well.

"Farewell my fellow goblins and other creatures, I will see all of you again someday. Goodbye," finished Fiddlin, as he hurried to the dragon with his own saddle.

* * *

The humans and Fiddlin took off on the dragon, to the one new land of Dormandian Necropolis. "Huh! What a quest that has been fulfilled," sighed Marcus. Suddenly, Robbert spotted a very odd-looking cave in the middle of the ocean. "Hey, what's that cave over there?" he asked. Everyone turned their heads to see the mysterious cave.

"Hmmm, very odd," said Fiddlin, looking at the map Lobje had returned to him. There was no sign of the cave on it. "This could be an ancient area…," continued Fiddlin, marking the cave on his map for another time.

And so, the humans continued on their journey towards their old school, itching to get back to their own dorm. All the boys wanted was some good food fit for humans, as last night they rested in the Stronghold chambers and had to eat the special burnt Relf lizards with burnt pig soup. Vlad wanted to get back to sword fighting, while Lyonis wanted to return to being a headmaster. Fiddlin, however, had no idea what he'd do till the next adventure they would have. Marcus suggested he enroll himself as a teacher at the school.

"You do know some useful spells, when the particular time arrives," he said, and that got Fiddlin to ponder it deeply. Lyonis said they will have the nightmare guard the lands along with the gold dragon, once he returns. "Till it is needed once more, which hopefully will not arise, it shall guard the school," he said, patting his steed.

The humans continued their long ride to the Dormandian land, even as night fell. "Well, that's the end of another great adventure…," said Marcus. Robbert said, "Aye, who knows, maybe it is to be the last of them…"

(It wasn't their last adventure)

THE END

Or is it? turn the page to find out…

27

A Really Short Chapter

Swoosh! Swoosh!

Out at sea, faraway from our heroes, a mysterious island lay still. The wind was whistling, and it was very cloudy. The island was very small, and was home to just two living things. Suddenly, one of them woke up. "Squeak! Hurr. W-what is this place?" It was a bat. A vampire bat. The bat turned around and saw the other living thing. "Master!" it said. "Welcome back, Scat the bat. That stupid dragon almost killed me, but no, we have speed-lighted," said the figure with its eyes closed.

"Gosh! My rocky remains must have been caught up in it! The magic brought me back to life," it said. "Yes, you were, old fiend" said the other figure. "Oh, I'll kill that blasted dragon and those two little children. The whole lot of them, for that matter! They killed our fellow vampires, sir!" it cried.

"It is alright." said the other dark figure, rising from the ground. "We are dreadfully close to Hell Fall. We will get our revenge and we will do much more destruction this time," said the figure, grinning. "We must now head to the forsaken pits, to create the greatest army ever to be known. We shall unite the dark hordes of hell!"

The black figure also turned into a bat, but much bigger.

"As you wish, s-sir... Drador." And the two bats flew off, swallowed up by the dark sky...

* * *

Hmmm, how very odd, I wonder where the vampire councilors have gotten to...

HEE, HEE, HAA, HAAR, HAAR! You'll just have to wait for the next book...

THE END

For real, not kidding this time...